Dream Angus

Alexander McCall Smith is the author of over fifty books, including the No. 1 Ladies' Detective Agency series of novels and several collections of short stories, including *The Girl Who Married a Lion* and *Heavenly Date and Other Flirtations*. Many of his books have become bestsellers throughout the world and he has received numerous awards for his writing, including the British Book Awards Author of the Year Award in 2004 and a CBE for Services to Literature in 2007. He lives in Scotland.

Dream Angus

Also by Alexander McCall Smith

Dream Angus

Alexander
McCall Smith

CANONGATE

This Canons edition published in 2019 by Canongate Books

First published in Great Britain in 2006 by Canongate Books Ltd,
14 High Street, Edinburgh EH1 1TE

canongate.co.uk

1

British Library Cataloguing-in-Publication Data
A catalogue record for this book is available on
request from the British Library

ISBN 978 1 78689 453 3

Typeset in Van Dijck by Palimpsest Book Production Ltd,
Falkirk, Stirlingshire

Printed and bound in Great Britain by Clays Ltd, Elcograf S.p.A.

For Malcolm and Nicola Wood

CONTENTS

Introduction

This story is a retelling of the myth of Angus, a popular and attractive figure of the Celtic mythology of Ireland and Scotland. Angus is a giver of dreams, an Eros, a figure of youth. He comes down to us from Irish mythology, but he is encountered, too, in Celtic Scotland. He is a benign figure – handsome and playful – who in modern times has inspired not only the poem of W.B. Yeats, 'The Song of Wandering Aengus', but also the lilting Scottish lullaby, 'Dream Angus'.

In this version of the story of Angus, although I have taken some liberties with the original, I have tried to maintain the central features of Angus's life as these are revealed to us in the Irish mythological sources. These sources, though, do not provide much detail, and so I have imagined what his mother, Boann, might be like; I have interpreted the character of his father, the Dagda, in a particular way and have deprived him of the definite article that precedes his name; I have assumed that

Bodb was rather overbearing. Purists may object to this, but myths live, and are there to be played with. At the same time, it is important to remind readers of the fact that if they want the medieval versions, unsullied by twenty-first-century inter-polation, they still exist, and are accessible. We must bear in mind, however, that those earlier texts are themselves reworked versions of things passed from mouth to mouth, embroidered and mixed up in the process. Myth is a cloud based upon a shadow based upon the movement of the breeze.

Celtic mythology is a rich and entrancing world, peopled by both mortals and gods. It embraces the notion of parallel universes, the real world and the otherworld. There are signs of the otherworld in the real world – mounds, hills and loughs – and the location of mythical places is frequently tied to real geographical features. It is no respecter of chronology, though, even if the later Irish heroic tales claim to have happened at a particular time in history. Angus belongs to the early body of stories – stories of a time beyond concrete memory.

★   ★   ★

INTRODUCTION

In retelling the story of Angus, I have brought him into the modern world in a series of connected stories which for the most part take place in modern Scotland. The part played by Angus, or the Angus figure, in each of these, may be elusive, but such a figure is present in each of them. Unlike some mythical figures, Angus does no particular moral or didactic work: he is really about dreams and about love – two things that have always had their mysteries for people. Angus puts us in touch with our dreams – those entities which Auden described so beautifully in his Freud poem as the creatures of the night that are waiting for us, that need our recognition. But Angus does more than that: he represents youth and the intense, passionate love that we might experience when we are young but which we might still try to remember as age creeps up. Age and experience might make us sombre and cautious, but there is always an Angus within us – Angus the dreamer.

Alexander McCall Smith, 2006

1

There was water

This happened in Ireland, but the memory of it is in Scotland too. The precise location of things was not so important then, as there was just the land and the sea between them, and people came and went between the lands, and they were brothers and sisters. The land itself was beautiful, with hills that ran down to the sea, and there were cold green waves that broke on the rocks that marked the edge of the land. There were islands, too, with stretches of white sand, and behind the white sand there was the machair, which was made up of meadows on which grew yellow and blue flowers, tiny flowers.

The gods lived everywhere then, and they moved among the people. But there were some gods who had their own place, and they were sometimes very powerful, as Dagda was. He was one of the great gods, and his people lived on islands at the very edge of the world, where there is just the blue of the sea and the west beyond the blue. They came to Ireland on a cloud, and lived there. Dagda was one of them, the good one, and he had great power, with his cauldron in which there was limitless food, and his great club, with which he could slay many men with a single blow. But he was often kind to men, and he could bring them back to life with the other end of the club. He also had fecund fruit trees which never stopped bearing fruit, and two remarkable pigs, one of which was always being cooked while the other was always growing.

There are many stories of Dagda and his doings. This one is about how he came to father a boy called Angus, and how Angus delighted all who came across him. In many ways, this was Dagda's greatest achievement, that he gave us this fine boy, who brought dreams to people, and who was loved by birds and people equally and who still is. For Dream Angus still comes at night and gives you dreams. You do not see him do this, but you may spot him skipping across the heather, his bag of dreams by his side, and the sight of him, just the sight, may be enough to make you fall in love. For he is also a dispenser of love, an Eros.

How was it that Dagda, a great and powerful god, a leader of warriors, should have had such a son? One might have thought, surely, that a god like that would have a son who was skilled in military matters, rather than a dreamer who fell in love and who was a charmer of birds. For an explanation of the gentleness of Angus, we must turn to his mother. She was a water spirit called Boann. Water spirits are gentle; their sons are handsome and have a sense of fun; they sparkle and dart about, just like water, which is the most playful of the elements.

Boann lived in a river. This was one of those rivers which was both great and small. There were places where its bed grew quite broad, and at such places one might walk across the river without getting even one's ankles wet. At other places there were pools, deep and dark, with water the colour of peat, and in these pools swam trout who lived for many years and had a great wisdom of matters pertaining to water and fish. Then there were places where the river was in-between – not deep, but not shallow. These were good places for water spirits to live.

Boann lived in one of these places. She was shy, as water spirits often are, and it was possible to walk right past the place where she was and not see her at all. All that you might see would be a ripple in the surface of the water, or a splash, perhaps, of the sort made by an otter or some other small creature slipping into the water, not enough to make you turn your head or think of investigating further.

Boann was gentle, and if, after rain, the river ran high, it was still always calm when it came to the place where she lived, as she would smooth the surface with her breath, which was like a soft, warm breeze. She was kind, too, and when a holy man came to the river's edge and asked whether he could lie down in the water, she readily agreed. She brought him some honey which she had and let him suck on the comb until it was drained of sweetness and all that was left were the wax cells of the bees.

That holy man was tired; he lay back in the water after he had sucked on the honey and he soon fell asleep. His head dropped beneath the surface, but he did not drown, as it is well known that holy men can live under a river even if ordinary men cannot. She watched over him, and saw that he was breathing peacefully, even though he was underwater.

This holy man was still there when morning came. Boann looked down through the water and saw that his eyes were open, and that he was staring up at her. She called to him, and he surfaced, coming up slowly through the clear water and breaking out into the air with a great shaking of his locks. She gave him another honeycomb, which again he sucked dry. Then he sank back beneath the water once more.

Sometimes the holy man spent all day under the river; on other occasions he would emerge from the water and walk off along one of the paths. He would talk to the people who were working in the fields and give them his blessings. They would give him food in return. They all knew that he lived under the river, but they were respectful of him, and they did not come to see him there. They knew, too, that Boann was looking after him and that they did not need to do anything for him other than listen politely when he spoke to them about things that they did not really understand.

The holy man told Boann many stories. For the most part these stories were about his boyhood and about the white dog which he had. This white dog had a brave heart, and did many fine deeds. Then he went away, and the holy man never saw him again, although he sometimes heard him barking in the distance. There were many stories of this sort, which Boann listened to, and each time the holy man told them they were different in some small detail. Sometimes the dog wore a collar of gold and sometimes it was a collar of leather. Sometimes the dog caught a hare, and sometimes he would pursue and capture a deer. Boann listened patiently to all these stories and occasionally at night she dreamed about a white dog, which she was convinced was the dog of the holy man's boy-hood.

Boann was pleased that the holy man had come to live under her river. She knew that the local people had seen him, and she knew that he was safe with them, but she did not want any gods to hear about him. It was not unknown for gods to become jealous of holy men, or to be possessive of them, and she did not want anybody to kill her holy man or take him away from her place in the river. So if ever any god came into that part of the country, Boann would tell the holy man to stay underwater until she called to him that it was safe to come out. She also acquired a bell which she would ring if she spotted a god. This was to be the warning signal to the holy man to get back into the water if he was sitting on the bank or walking in the fields.

Boann was, of course, very beautiful, although very few men had seen her face. Eventually word reached Dagda that there was a graceful water spirit living in that river and he decided that he would see whether her beauty was as striking as was reported. He picked up his club and set off towards the river. The sun was high in the sky and his shadow was short. Nobody would know that Dagda was coming, because he was the wind and the rain and the clouds in the sky. Dagda was Ireland, and Ireland was all about. He was Scotland too, and lands beyond that.

When he came to the river he saw Boann sitting upon a rock. She was singing to the holy man, who had come up out of the water and was drying his hair in the sun. Dagda stopped and listened to the song that Boann was singing. It was very beautiful – like the sound of running water. He was, of course, immensely jealous, and he decided that he would kill the holy man as soon as the opportunity presented itself.

Boann had to go to another place to see her husband, Elcmar. She had not thought of gods who might be watching; she had not thought of Dagda.

Dagda saw Boann set off, and he puffed out his cheeks and blew a wind which would help her on her journey. Then he waited. Now there was nobody about, nobody who would see him on his murderous errand. Laying down his great club, he strode across to the edge of the river and looked down into the water. There was the holy man, staring up at him, wondering who it was who had seen fit to disturb his retreat.

Dagda laughed. A holy man was no match for him, and he reached down into the water, his great forearm making small waves, his blunt fingers snatching at the holy man below. Then he pulled him out of the water, shook him, and held him high up in the sky, as one would hold up a fish one had caught so that others might admire it. The holy man could not breathe up there. All about him was sky and more sky, and he struggled and gasped, his thin cries lost in the rushing wind that was Dagda's breath. It was to no avail; he drowned in the sky, and after he died, as a fish will die in the air, his eyes were wide, as the eyes of a fish will be, and his skin turned to scales. The light was silver on these scales – silver and gold, like the scales of a trout when it is taken from sweet water. Dagda then tossed the body of the holy man away, and it cart-wheeled across the sky before it fell.

Dagda now put on the holy man's clothes, which had slipped off him when he died. Then, entering the water, he sank below the surface, making his face and his hair look like the face and hair of the holy man. There he waited for Boann to come back from her journey.

At sunset the next day she returned. Dagda lay quite still as she settled for the night, but when the stars were out and all was quiet he called to her from under the river, and he called her in the voice of the holy man. Boann arose from her bed of reeds and crossed the river in the darkness, going to the place where the holy man lived. Dagda, now revealed, was waiting for her and he held her in his arms and she immediately conceived of a child. Boann was secretly pleased by this, as she had been in love with Dagda but had been frightened by what her husband would think if she were to be seen in the company of the powerful god. Fortunately, her husband had been sent off on an errand by Dagda, who had also made time stand still for him for a period of nine months – the time during which Boann would be bearing Dagda's child.

Dagda, however, did not intend to stay with Boann. He was already married and had to return to his own wife. He went away, laughing so loudly that people woke up and thought that there had been thunder, and were frightened.

2

His child grew within her

Boann was filled with anger that she had been tricked in this way by Dagda. For several days she lay in the river weeping – weeping for the humiliation which the god had visited upon her and weeping, too, for the holy man, whose fate she had heard about from a man who had seen what had happened. She had loved the holy man, and she missed his undemanding company and his often-repeated stories about his boyhood. But she knew that soon she would have a child and that this child would keep her company and make up for the loss of her friend. So she did not mourn for long.

She went to see her husband, who was in a distant part of the country. She found him standing on a rock at the entrance to a valley. He was perfectly still, one arm raised as if he were about to point at something; but the gesture never came, as

Dagda had frozen him. Boann spoke to him, addressing him as her husband, but he did not respond. Even when she shouted to him that she had been taken by Dagda, he did not respond. It was as if all his senses had gone to sleep and nothing could awaken him.

Boann carried Elcmar back to her river and stood him by the side of a field. People took him offerings of food in the evening, leaving them at his perfectly immobile feet. The next day the offerings were not there. People pointed to this and said that it showed that Elcmar was eating, although he only ate late at night when there was nobody about to see him. In fact, the food was being eaten by large rats, who passed by that way each night and were delighted to find a source of good food. The only person who could have seen this happening was Elcmar, and he could see nothing, because his eyes could not move: not the pupils, not the muscles within the ball of the eyes, not the eyelids. Nothing could move.

Boann felt Dagda's child growing within her. She

had not had a child before and she found the experience a strange and exciting one. As the months wore on, she became heavier and heavier, and rarely left her place in the river. The fish, who had been wary of her when she was quick in the water, now swam up to her with impunity, staring at her with their unblinking eyes, moving slowly in the current of the river, watching her. Some of the fish brought her food, which they found further down the river, gently nudging it into her hand, waiting for her to grasp it before they swam off. Boann was grateful for this, and she remembered the names of those fish who had helped her, writing them down in a book which she had with her.

When her time came, she moved slowly out of the water and lay upon the bank. From the river, the fish watched her silently; a great number of them had now assembled, and they gazed at her with wonder as she lay under the sky, looking up into the blue, the sun upon her hair and brow, like gold.

There was silence, just silence. Then she let out

a great cry and Angus was born. At that moment, a great flock of birds that had alighted in the nearby trees rose up in a cloud and wheeled and dipped through the morning sky. In the river the fish swam rapidly this way and that and some leaped out of the water, describing half circles in the air before falling back again with a great splash.

Angus looked at Boann with his blue eyes. She kissed him gently and held him in her arms with all the tenderness of a mother. She knew that this was a child who would be filled with love and who would bring that love to all who saw him. She knew that. She wanted the world to see him, to share in her pride, but she knew that this was not possible. She would have to hide him, as Dagda would steal him if he heard that she had borne him a son. So she made a basket for him, a small cradle, out of the rushes that grew there. Angus slept in this cradle, which floated on the edge of the river, and was watched over while he slept by Boann, who was never far away. Her husband was still in his enchanted coma, but was beginning to show stirrings of life now – the twitching of a muscle here, the almost imperceptible movement of a limb there; small signs that he would not be asleep forever.

There were a number of remarkable things which happened now. One of these was the appearance around the infant's head of small birds, of many different colours. These birds came from the hedgerows and from the trees, and took turns in circling Angus as he lay in his basket. At first Boann tried to shoo them away, fearing that they would disturb the baby's sleep, but when she saw that they did not do this, and that Angus slept soundly even as the birds sang, she left them unmolested.

Other things happened. People began to have vivid dreams. One woman who lived not far from the place where Angus was born had for many years hoped for a child, but none had come. She and her husband were wealthy in other ways, but she had remained barren. She began to dream that she had a child, and every night this child appeared to her in her dreams, growing each time from being so tiny as to be almost invisible, until it was the same size as a normal baby. She mentioned these dreams to her husband, who smiled and said, 'That is a dream baby and it is not a real baby at all.' But she knew differently, and each night she knew that she would meet the baby in her dreams and would care for him. Then one night the dream baby said to her, 'It is time for me to be born, mother', and when she awoke there was a baby beside her, and he was the same baby who had appeared to her in her dreams.

'Do not talk about this thing,' her husband warned her. 'People will not believe you if you tell them that this is a dream baby.'

The woman remained silent and nobody knew that her baby had arrived in this way. But they knew that she was happy.

Although Boann took every care to make sure that Dagda did not hear of the birth of Angus, it was inevitable that the news should reach him. Only a few days after Angus had been born, Dagda heard from one of his men that Boann had built a cradle. This man had seen her pick the reeds for the cradle from the river bank and had immediately reported the matter. Dagda smiled. 'I have a son,' he said.

Creeping out of his house, his great club in his hand, Dagda made his way to a small hill that over-looked the river. There he hid behind a large tree, and his club appeared from a distance to be no more than an extra branch of that tree and his hair was the leaves of the tree. He stood there for a whole day, waiting until Boann should come out of the river and reveal where Angus was hidden.

Dagda waited. There were clouds in the sky and there was rain; there were black cattle that moved across the hillside; there was a deer in the high grass; there were swans which came from the west and flew low over the river. But Dagda did not move.

At last Boann appeared from the water, singing a song that she liked to sing to Angus. From his hill Dagda watched her walk to the place where Angus's cradle was hidden. He watched as she picked him up and held him to her. The god's eyes were bright, and with a great roar he came from the tree and strode down the hillside and snatched Angus from his mother. Boann struggled, but she was water. She pleaded with Dagda not to take her child, but her pleading was no more than the sound that a river makes when it crankles between stones. She called to her husband to help her, but it was like calling to one who is not there, or to one who is dead. She wept, but her tears were no more than the soft rain which fell when Angus had gone from her sight.

After the kidnapping of Angus, Boann's husband awoke from his long sleep. He opened his eyes and looked about him. In his mind it was the same day as it had been before, and it was as if he had only been sleeping for a few minutes. He saw his wife, and smiled at her. He saw the cradle in which Angus had been laid, but thought that it was just a basket that his wife had made while he was sleeping.

Boann watched him. He did not know, and she could not tell him. She could weep for the child she had lost, her beautiful child, but she could not let her husband see her tears. Her husband was puzzled at her sadness, but he decided that she must simply have had a bad dream — such things happened, and he knew that people could cry if they woke from a bad dream. He put his arms around her to comfort her, but she was water.

3

That was then; this is now.
But he is still here.

He put his arms about her, gently, with love. It was a time of embraces.

'Sleep?' he said. 'I saw your eyes close when we were on the ferry. Halfway across from Skye, you went to sleep. I saw you.'

She smiled. 'It was warm. The air was very heavy in there. Why do they have no windows in those boats?'

'You don't want windows in the winter,' he said. 'That's why.'

She sat on the edge of the bed and smoothed the counterpane under her hand. Somebody had taken the trouble to embroider the linen, to work a design with tiny, careful stitches. It must have been a while ago, when there was time for such things. She looked around the room, at their suitcase that the owner of the small hotel had brought in for them and had placed on a rickety stand near the window, at the window itself, and the green hills of the island outside. It seemed so strange to be here, with him, with this man whom she knew, but did not really know, her husband now.

She rose and went to the window, peering out over the small lawn. At the edge of the lawn, between the hotel grounds and the single-track road that ran down the island, was a dry-stane dyke, one of those mortarless walls of rough-hewn stone, lichen-covered, sturdy against the years and the weather. On a twisted strand of wire, tufts of sheep's wool had been caught, and these were tugged at by the wind. Her gaze wandered on, past the road, to the field beyond – a field which ended in dunes, the sand appearing at first in little scars on the grass, and then the sand proper and the bay.

He stood beside her at the window, looking out. She felt the side of his arm against her, and the warmth from that through her blouse. He said, 'We can go for a walk down there before we have dinner. There's time. You're not too tired, are you?'

'Of course not.' She retrieved a sweater from the suitcase and slipped it over her head. For a moment she saw just the dark of the wool and then, her head emerging from the neck, she saw that he was watching her. She blushed; it was part of the intimacy of marriage that these little things, dressing and undressing, looking in the mirror, unconscious gestures, should be observed; it was the end of privacy.

They left their room and walked down the corridor towards the front door. The hotel had been a manse and was not large – no more than six bedrooms, a dining room, and a drawing room to the front. The owner was in the drawing room with his wife, she slipping the menu for the evening into a leather folder, he bending down to feed a log on to the fire in the hearth. Although it was summer, the evenings could be chilly enough for a fire inside. He looked up as they went past and smiled.

Outside, the evening sun was low on the hills

behind the small cluster of houses around the hotel. There were gulls in the air and several perched on the wall, their mews sharp and strident, protesting. He took her hand in his and they crossed the road together and climbed over the fence at the other side. Now they were on the machair, and the wind was from the sea, bringing iodine and salt and the coconut smell of gorse, which was in bloom at the edge of the fields.

They climbed over the low dunes and ran down together on to the beach. He lifted up a strand of seaweed from the high-tide mark, unravelling it from a tangled skein of rope. There were the shattered spars of fish boxes, driftwood, whitened shells; the detritus of the oceans. He spun the seaweed round in an arc, and again, and let it fly out of his hand up into the air. She picked up a shell and blew the sand off it, revealing the intricate patterns, ridges, coruscations. When she was a girl she had blown the fluff off dandelions, one puff for each letter of the alphabet, representing the first letter of the name of the man she would marry, the man

who would come and take her away from the nar-
rowness, the constraints, of home. She glanced at
him, at his hair ruffled in the wind, and thought,
And it was him all along.

They walked along the beach, following the line
of the retreating tide where the sand, still damp,
was firmer underfoot. There was nobody about and
out to sea there were no boats, nothing. She said,
'All the way to America. That way. All the way to
America. And Canada.'

He followed her gaze. 'Yes,' he said. 'Ireland is
a bit to the south – over there. And Greenland, I
suppose.'

'I'm getting cold,' she said. 'Can we go back?'

'Of course.'

She looked at him. One of the surprising things
in all this, she thought, is the sheer otherness. He
is another person; he is not me. And there is a bit
of him, of what makes him himself, which I shall
never know, never touch. Something which I don't
know the word for. The soul? No. Well, maybe.
That, whatever it is, will never be mine. What if I

were to ask him to tell me some secret about himself; no secret in particular, just one that he would
never tell anybody else, not ever. All of us have at
least one of those. At least one secret. She smiled
at the thought. What would she tell him if he asked
her the same question? What had she done, or
thought; what would she *like* to do, or think, if she
were to allow herself?

She thought about this as they walked back across
the machair and crossed the road. Before them was
the white shape of the hotel, its high windows
catching the last of the evening sun, reflecting now
the empty sky, a shimmer of blue and silver. There
was gravel underfoot on the uneven surface of the
drive, filling in the potholes that were made by the
rainwater when it lay. The unmistakeable smell of
peat was in the air, which reminded her of family
holidays, when she was young, and they would travel
up from Gourock to stay near Fort William, and that
smell would drift over from a small farmhouse
nearby.

★   ★   ★

'Honeymoon couple,' whispered a middle-aged woman in the dining room, and they overheard it and she blushed. He grinned at her as they sat down at their table and they tried to avoid looking at the table from which the remark had come. But it was difficult, as there were only six tables in the room, and she eventually looked and smiled back at the woman, who smiled at her coyly.

The hotel prided itself on its culinary reputation and at the end of the dinner the owner, who had cooked, came out of the kitchen wearing his white apron and spoke to everybody about what they had eaten. Then they went through to the drawing room, where a tray of coffee and pieces of broken Scottish tablet had been laid out. She picked up a magazine and paged through it while he spoke to one of the other guests about fishing. This man had been on all the local lochs and knew which flies worked where. It was a dull conversation for her, too masculine, and she concentrated on her magazine. But she still found herself thinking, *What if he did have a secret? Would he tell me? Would I want to know?*

They did not stay long. The other guests went to their rooms; the ceiling in the drawing room creaked as somebody upstairs crossed the floor; this was an old house. Their room, being at the side of the house away from the evening sun, had become chilly, and she shivered as she undressed. He stood by the window and said, 'Let's leave the curtains open. I love this night light here. What do the Russians say? White nights?' Then he said, 'I want to go for a walk. Do you want to come?'

She was already in bed. She felt tired, rather drowsy. She shook her head. 'You go.'

'It's just that I love it when it's dark, but not really dark. And the wind has dropped. It's very still outside.'

'You go.'

She turned off the light when he had gone and closed her eyes. She thought that being in this air made her tired; something to do with ozone perhaps. She always felt tired when she first came to places like this. Perhaps it was the quiet. Perhaps it was being here, on the very edge of Scotland, that made her feel different; because everything was in fact different – the light, the people, the sky; different and somehow magical, as if a distinctive physics applied.

She drifted off to sleep and then back, half awake, half asleep, into drowsy consciousness. He had come back into the room. He was a figure silhouetted against the dusky light of the window, a chiaroscuro effect. He came round to her side of the bed and bent down beside her, his face close to hers. She murmured, mumbled, eyes half closed, lips barely moving. 'Your walk . . .'

He whispered something into her ear, something she did not hear properly, but which she felt she understood, had taken in. She struggled with sleep, willing herself back from the darkness, but she was very tired. She saw, dimly, that he walked lightly round to the other side of the room and then opened the door and went out. Why was he going out again? He had been for his walk and had come back. Why would he go out again?

Then the light was turned on, and she woke up properly.

'Where did you go?' she asked.

'Along the road,' he said. 'It goes on for miles.'

'No,' she said. 'When you came back a few minutes ago. You went out again.'

He looked at her, puzzled. 'I didn't come back just a few minutes ago. This is the first time. I've just come back. Now.'

She sat up in bed. 'You came in,' she said. 'You whispered something to me. I was half asleep.'

He laughed. 'I didn't! You must have been dreaming.'

She was adamant. 'No,' she said, her voice rising. 'There was a man. He came in. He stood at the side of the bed. I'm not imagining it.'

He looked concerned now. 'Are you sure?'

'Positive.'

He was silent for a moment. 'I'm going to lock the door.' He turned and went towards the door. Then he stopped. 'No, I'm going to have a word with the owner. What did he look like, this man? Can you describe him?'

She could not. 'But it wasn't you,' she said.

He went out. He thought that the owner and his wife were still in the kitchen, as a light shone from under the door and there was the low murmur of voices. He knocked and the owner opened it, looking surprised.

'Yes. Is there anything . . . ?'

'There was a stranger in our room. My wife saw him.'

The owner turned round and looked at his wife, who came over to join them, wiping her hands on kitchen towel. There was steam coming from a basin behind her. A kettle whistled.

'A stranger?' she asked. She had the accent of the island, the old voice, the music.

He nodded. 'Yes. He came to the bedside,' he said. 'I wasn't there. I was out for a walk.'

The owner exchanged glances with his wife. He whispered something to her under his breath.

'What was that?' He had not heard clearly, but it sounded like, *She saw Angus.*

'Nothing,' said the owner. 'Nothing. I really don't know. It might have been one of the other

— 33 —

guests, do you think? One of the other guests going to the bathroom along the corridor and getting the doors mixed up? That has happened, you know.'

'An intruder?' he said. It was a sinister word; all wrong in this place.

The owner shook his head. 'Very unlikely. Not here. No.'

The stood in silence for a while. Then, 'Well, I'm going to have to lock the door.'

The owner nodded. 'Of course. Of course.'

He went back to the bedroom. She was lying back in bed again, but looked wide awake now. This was not surprising, he thought, as it must have been a shock. And he felt a bit guilty, too, that he had not been in the room when it happened.

She lay awake for some time. He dropped off to sleep, but she lay there, aware of the attenuated light outside, the faint glow that seemed to come from the hills. Then drowsiness overcame her and she drifted off to sleep. To dreams.

She dreamed of his secret.

4

The childhood of Angus

Dagda carried his son back, proud of him, of the pretty child in his arms. The birds which had kept Angus company had begun to follow him, but they were frightened off by the god's giant strides and the sight of his great club. So there was no bird-song to accompany Angus on this journey; just the sound of Dagda's footfall and the rasping of his breath. Angus was silent; he did not cry, but looked up at the man who was carrying him, his gaze fixed on the face of the man who had taken him from his mother.

Angus spent one night at Dagda's house, sleeping in the kitchen, near that large cauldron, with the women who kept the fires burning. They made sure that he was comfortable and that he was well settled before they retired to their own beds on the floor near the fire. That night all of them dreamed vivid dreams, waking in the morning wide-eyed with wonder at the things they had seen in these dreams, astonishing things, wonderful things.

One of the women said, 'I dreamed last night that I was in a land where women were not the property of men. The men stayed at home and did all the hard work which women do; the cooking, the cleaning, the watching of children – men did all that. Women ruled the land in my dream, and they did not spend their time raiding other people's cattle or destroying their houses. They ruled gently, like women.'

The other women looked at each other in astonishment. They had all had strange dreams, but none had dreamed of so wondrous a thing as that.

Dagda dreamed too, and when he appeared in the kitchen that morning he gruffly ordered the women to take Angus to the house of Midir, his son, where he would be raised as Midir's own child. He had decided that he did not want to keep Angus in his house, as even though Angus was still a babe in arms he had already revealed his qualities. Besides, Dagda felt threatened. He had none of the charm that Angus had, and he sensed that a clever, attractive son would be a threat to him when they both grew older. And Dagda had dreamed that night, too, and in his dream he had seen a fair-haired boy knocking at the door of his house and gently leading him outside. Once he was outside, he was alone and without his men to guard him and without his cauldron. But what was worse, was that his club, that great club of his, was weak and useless, a limp thing that could neither smite nor terrify. That was the real nightmare, and Dagda had woken from it filled with dread and anxiety.

The women took Angus away, wrapping him in a blanket for the journey. No sooner had they left Dagda's house, than the small birds which had previously flown about Angus's head returned. The women were astonished by this, but they were not frightened, because these birds were gentle and wanted only to sing to Angus and to delight in his company.

Midir was pleased to receive the infant. He gave him a room in his house and this room had a window at which the small birds could wait while Angus was inside. Two women were given the job of looking after him, and they were both known for their kindness. They held Angus gently and sang to him at night, soothing him off to sleep with old songs that they remembered from their own childhood. And when Angus was fretful and could not sleep, they took him into bed with them, under thick, warm skins, and cuddled him until he dropped off to sleep. On such occasions, when Angus slept in their beds, the women found that they dreamed very intensely – strange dreams from which they awoke feeling elated, as if they had seen things that only gods might normally see. One woman dreamed of a cow that gave cream, rather than milk; another dreamed of a river that flowed backwards, in from the sea, which was filled with succulent mussels, sweet to the taste, as thick as the fist of a man.

They thought it strange that they should have

these dreams only when Angus was sleeping with them, but stranger than that, surely, was something which one of the women noticed about the birds that perched at Angus's window overnight, waiting until he should come outside in the morning. At first the women thought that these birds never truly slept, as they made tiny sounds, chirruping through the night, but then they noticed that the birds' eyes were indeed closed and that the sounds they made were the sounds of their bird-dreams, as a sleeping dog will growl when it chases some quarry in its dreams. Nobody had imagined that birds dreamed, and many would have said it was impossible, for birds have very small heads and there is no room for dreams in such heads; but these women now knew differently, because they had seen it. They knew that birds had dreams, even if these dreams were tiny ones, of small things that happened, in small places – amongst the leaves, or in little corners, in the small lives of birds.

Angus grew quickly. It did not take him long to

learn how to walk, and then how to run. Soon he was going out by himself, just a small boy, but one who could skip and dart across the turf as nimbly as if he were a deer. Indeed he could run with the deer, who did not seem to mind his being beside them, and it was a fine sight to see him with those fleet creatures, keeping at their side, effortlessly bounding across the hillsides.

Angus did not care about danger. If any peril threatened him, the birds about his head would warn him with their cries, and they would even try to head danger off, swooping down on anything that could harm the boy. But for the most part they did not have to do this, as there was something about Angus that pacified otherwise dangerous creatures.

Midir had hunting dogs – large creatures that howled and brayed and tore at their prey with fearsome teeth. These dogs lived in an enclosure into which even the bravest huntsman was loath to venture – but Angus did. One day when he was still very small he went into this place before anybody could stop him. The woman who was watching over him had turned her head for the briefest of moments, and in that small space of time Angus had made his way into the dogs' cage.

When she saw what had happened, the woman let out a howl of anguish and rushed to the enclosure gate. She called out to Angus, and sought to distract the hunting dogs so that they should not see him. But the dogs paid no attention to her, and bounded over to the boy, snapping their jaws at the birds as they dipped in protective flight about them. The woman's heart stopped within her: Angus was bound to be ripped to pieces by those savage creatures, just as they would tear a hare limb from limb, before a huntsman could even get near them.

She need not have worried. As they approached Angus, the dogs began to quieten, and soon they dropped onto their haunches, and lay, their tongues across their teeth, their heads lowered in submission. Whimpering, they went to the boy and licked his hands and feet and even his face, while he laughed in delight at the feel of the dogs' rough attentions. Thereafter, the dogs grew quiet whenever he was around, and liked nothing more than to stand at his side, ready for the hunt.

Everything he did, he did very well, and Midir was proud of him. He never told Angus that he was Dagda's son, and so the growing boy believed that Midir was his true father, and he loved him as a son should love his father. And he loved, too, the other boy who was the son of Midir and therefore his brother – or so he believed.

This brother was older than Angus, and he could do many of the things that Angus could do, although he could not bring dreams to people and he could not attract birds to fly around his head. But he was a fine boy, too, and when people saw the two boys together they remarked how good a thing it was that two brothers should be such friends. Such a friendship, they said, could last all one's life, and could be the source of great joy and comfort.

But when he was eight years old, Angus dreamed

that he would lose his brother. He awoke in tears; he saw that his brother was there, but he was not there.

5

My brother

It was not much of a village — just a few white-painted cottages along a small road that went nowhere important. In summer, people came to stay at the big house up the glen — well-off people from Edinburgh, who didn't mix very much with the local people but who at least brought some jobs for a few months of the year. His father worked a little for those people; he mended the roof of the house one year and on another occasion he spent two months fixing the road that led to their favourite fishing spot — it had been washed away in several places by heavy rains which had put the burn into spate. They helped him — both boys; their job was to collect stones which he could use to make a firm base for the repairs. They would collect these in large, unwieldy baskets which he told them their grandfather had used for fish. The boys found scales in the wickerwork, the scales of long-dead salmon.

Their house was at the far end of the village, a bit beyond the village really, on a track which meandered along the lower contours of the big hill. That hill was one which locals did not like to go up because they knew that something bad had happened there, something a long time ago, at the time of the Jacobite rising, the Forty-Five, when people had been thrown out of their homes and the Gaelic language itself and the kilt had been declared an enemy of the authorities. Nobody remembered exactly what had happened, but they knew where it had happened – somewhere up there.

Not that this put off the climbers and walkers who came from elsewhere. They met in the village, parking their cars on the verge of the road beside the general store, unfolding maps and looking up at the hill, pointing at possible approaches. He watched them set off, and they would nod to him, or give him a boiled sweet from their pockets. He was too shy to speak to them, but he watched them with that clear intensity of expression that accompanies innocence.

'Look at that boy's eyes,' whispered a woman to her husband, keen climbers both; rucksacks bulging with bad-weather gear, sandwiches, a spirit stove.

'Classic Highlander. That's how they breed them here.'

He was Jamie, the younger one, and his brother, who was older, sixteen, was Davey. People could tell that they were brothers; they had the same clear skin, the same mop of dark hair that went with those blue eyes – Celtic colouring, people said. Women could not resist ruffling their hair, which embarrassed both of them; the younger one because he thought that at eleven he was too old for that; the older one because he found it shameful that older women should look at males that way.

For Jamie, the arc that described the universe, the informing principle, the very reason for existence was his brother. He wanted to be his brother, but could not; then he would be as close as he could to that. He tried to walk like this brother, to throw his hair back from his forehead like his brother, to scoop a trout out of one of the pools in the burn just as his brother did, ankle-deep in peaty water, looking down on the shape of the trout as it wriggled against the current of the water.

Davey good-naturedly tolerated this hero-worship. He knew that it was not easy to be the youngest in the family – there were two older sisters who had gone to Glasgow and who worked in a factory there, still, although everybody else seemed to be losing their jobs in this depression. It would end next year, in 1934, some said, when things would get better; but others said that it would not end that way, that it was the last stage of a rotten system and would be swept away when the people, the people who actually worked, asserted themselves. Their father did not believe this.

'Oh yes?' he said. 'And then who runs things? Jock Tamson?' Jock Tamson was a Scottish Everyman figure, the average man. He could not run a country nor an economy, said their father.

At least they ate well enough, which was more

than many who lived in the cities did. In Glasgow there were children who went to bed hungry, said their mother; every night. Here, at least, there was always fish, which could be had by the bucketful out in the bay; fast-running mackerel which could be salted or smoked, or eaten fresh, sea trout, flounder. And there were sheep from their grandmother's croft, and the eggs from their own chickens, and milk from their aunt's cow. Nobody was hungry here, but there was still no money for shoes – Jamie had none, and Davey had an old pair of his father's which let in the damp through a hole in one of the soles. 'Better than nothing,' said Davey, smiling 'Better than nae shoes at all.'

Jamie wore his brother's clothes – cast-offs which had been handed down by some other boy before Davey owned them. Their mother said that Davey was hard on his clothes, and she had to darn and mend them before they were passed on to Jamie. There was no shame in cast-offs – everybody wore them, even adults, and why waste money, which was so hard to come by, on new clothes?

And they shared a bed, too, the two brothers, as most children did in those days, in that place; a bed in a sleeping compartment off the kitchen; a recess with a thick coir mattress and a blanket for a curtain. It was a warm place to be, because the kitchen range was kept going with peat and wood, both of which were plentiful, and they could work up a good heat if the windows were kept firmly closed and nobody allowed the outside door to be left open. In summer it was too warm, and they slept with the curtain open to allow for circulation of air.

Davey taught him so much. He taught him how to read the currents when they took their father's rowing boat out through the mouth of the sea loch and into open water. There were currents that you had to watch if you wanted to avoid getting swept out to sea. In a few hours you could be halfway to Ireland, he said, if you weren't careful. Men did drown – they both knew that – because they had seen the funerals and they knew the fatherless bairns, as they called them, for whom a particular pity was felt. To be a fatherless bairn meant that you had nobody to put food on the table, and the parish would have to step in, or the family would have to go off somewhere where the children might get some work on a farm or something of that nature. Some boys ended up going off as far as Fife, to the pits, and leading their lives in the darkness, amongst those hard, alien people. That would be like dying, he thought.

They got into trouble once with the sea, and all their rowing seemed to get them nowhere. They were carried out further and further by a rip that snaked far out into deep water, the shore getting smaller by the moment and the waves choppier. The boat was taking on water, and Davey gave Jamie the baling can while he struggled with the oars; the can cut into his fingers and the salt stung the cuts, but he continued; and then the wind shifted, suddenly, and swept them back to land.

Davey laughed. He made light of things like that, and said, 'You didn't think I'd let us get carried away down to Skye, did you? I knew the wind would change. I knew it fine.'

'You didn't.'

'All right I didn't. But we're not drowned are we? No, we aren't.'

He looked at his brother in admiration. If he were not here, then all sorts of terrible things would happen to him. He would really drown then, because he would never be able to row back like that. And he would be bullied, too, if his brother were not there to protect him. There were boys who were bigger who liked to bully those who had no older brothers.

'You'll never go away, will you, Davey? You won't go away to Glasgow or anywhere?'

Davey looked at him oddly. 'Why would I be going to Glasgow?'

'To get a job.'

Davey scoffed. 'Who needs a job? I could do anything, anything.' He hesitated a little. 'But I don't want to.'

He was reassured by this. Davey would stay and keep him safe and they would live there, in that house, until their parents died and had been buried, and then they would divide the house in two and he would live in one end and Davey in the other and that would last forever. That is what he thought.

It started with a letter. The owner of the local store, who acted as postman, came up the track after lunch and gave the letter to his father. Jamie saw from the stamp that it was a letter from overseas. 'Canada,' his father said, and there was anxiety in his voice. Before he opened it, he let his son examine the stamp. 'You can tear it off the envelope later,' he said. 'Not now. Later.'

His father went into the kitchen to read the letter together with his mother. Jamie sensed that he should not go with him; they would tell him later on what the letter said, and of course he would have the stamp.

Then Davey came home. He had been helping with the painting of a boat, and there were flecks of white paint on his fingers and forearm.

'There's been a letter,' Jamie said to his brother.

'Oh yes?'

'From Canada.'

'Oh yes?'

That was all that was said between them. Davey had to wash his hands, to get the paint off, and he filled a basin with water and started to scrub with carbolic soap. Then his father came into the room and stopped when he saw Davey, as if thinking about something. He looked at Davey, frowned, though not at him, and seemed on the point of saying something, but did not. He walked out of the house.

'There's something in the letter,' Jamie said.

'Of course there is. You wouldn't get a letter with nothing in it.'

He came to his brother's side and watched him soaping his hands and scrubbing with the small wooden nailbrush. 'There's something about you in it,' he said.

Davey put down the brush and examined his hands. The paint was recalcitrant. 'Why would there be something about me in a letter from Canada? I've got nothing to do with Canada.'

Jamie persisted. 'I can tell. It was the way he looked at you. I can tell.'

His brother said nothing.

That night they heard their parents talking. They talked late into the night, as Jamie woke up at midnight and he could tell that they were still awake, a light coming from under their door, and the murmur of voices. In the morning, his father took Davey aside, put his arm over his shoulder, and led him out of the house to the place where the washing line was, on the grass at the back. He talked with the boy there, his arm still on his shoulder, pacing backwards and forwards. And from within the house, watching, the younger boy saw the two men – for his brother, surely, was almost a man – walking past the washing which his mother had hung out first thing that morning to catch the good weather. She had washed their father's dark suit, the one he wore to the kirk, and it was hanging, arms extended, as if in surrender. The breeze was in it and the arms were filled with air, the jacket billowing.

They came inside, and he studied Davey's face. There was a light in his eyes, an excitement.

'What was it?' he whispered. 'What was it?'

'Whisht,' said Davey. 'Later. I'll tell you later. Not now.'

He waited – an agony of waiting – and at mid-morning Davey said that he was going out to the sea-loch in the boat. There were crab pots there that needed to be checked; Jamie could come with him if he liked. They went straight out. The sun was on the water of the sea loch. The wind had died down, almost to nothing; the water was still.

Davey stopped rowing. 'That letter,' he said. 'There's a cousin in Canada. You don't know him. I don't know him. Father does.'

He stared at Davey, trying to read his expression. His brother was smiling.

'I'm going to Canada,' said Davey. 'I'm going to live there. He's paying my fare from Glasgow. He's taking me in, this cousin, and getting me a job in Halifax. That's in Canada.'

Jamie looked into the water beside the boat. Then

he looked up at his brother, and saw the scar on his leg where he had ripped the flesh on a piece of barbed wire two months ago. He saw that there was still some paint on his fingers; that the skin of the hands was brown, from the sun, from the wind, but there were still specks of white paint. And he wanted to disbelieve what he had just heard because so few words could not end a world.

He said, 'I'll come too, Davey. I'll come with you.'

And Davey shook his head. 'No, you can't come. You're too wee. Maybe when you're my age. Maybe then.'

They dragged up the crab pots in silence. From between the twisted bars of the pots there came a waving claw; black eyes on stalks; an undersized lobster. He felt the salt tears in his eyes, and was silent. Canada. Forever.

That night, unable to contain his sorrow, he burst into tears at the kitchen table. His brother lowered his head, his parents moved over to comfort him. He was immersed in his mother, pressed against the familiar texture of the jersey that she wore, old wool rubbed smooth. 'My poor bairn,' she whispered. 'You'll see Davey again. It's for the best. He'll have a grand life out there. A grand life.'

'There's nothing for him here,' said his father. 'Canada is such a big country. There are great chances there. This is the best thing for Davey. Do you think that we'd let him go otherwise? Do you think so?'

He had no answers for these questions. He was mute. And later, when their parents had gone to their room and they were alone in the kitchen, preparing for bed, he said to his brother, 'I'm going to run away. I'm going to follow you.'

'You can't do that, Jamie. You wouldn't even get as far as Fort William.'

He shook his head. He could try.

They lay on the coir mattress, the curtains of the sleeping compartment open. He could tell that Davey was not asleep; he could tell by his breathing. In the darkness his brother was just a shape under the coarse hodden blanket; the brother he loved more than anything in the world. His brother.

He reached out and took Davey's hand. Davey pressed the younger boy's fingers in his palm, squeezed the hand, which felt so dry and warm. The love between the brothers was deep.

'Try to go to sleep, Jamie,' he said. 'Maybe Angus will bring you dreams.'

'Angus?'

'Dream Angus. You've heard of him, haven't you? The laddie who brings dreams. Louping across the heather with his dreams.'

He said nothing. He snuggled up against his brother. 'I don't want you to go,' he whispered.

'Angus will bring you dreams about me in Canada,' said Davey drowsily. 'I'll ask him.'

Jamie said nothing. He heard his brother's breathing – a sound that had always comforted him, just as the sound of the sea had done. He closed his eyes. He dreamed of a place where there was snow, and forests stretching into the distance, the trees black against the snow. This place was Canada.

6

Angus finds out that his father is not his father

They played on the grass. Angus, who was the strongest and the fastest of the boys, led one group of youths, who wore upon their shirts the brooch of his side. They shouted to one another, words of encouragement, words of dismay at missed chances, urging others to run faster, to outwit the other group. Many people stood about, having stopped to admire the players, but in particular to witness the speed and agility of Angus. They had never seen a boy so fleet of foot, so beautiful in the way he moved.

Angus was a good-natured player, but it was inevitable that there should be moments when tempers were frayed. At one such moment, when a boy from the other side pushed him rudely and addressed harsh words to him, Angus said to him,

'I do not think it right that I should be spoken to like that, especially by the son of a slave.'

These words pricked the other boy, even if he had started the fight. Standing up to Angus he said, 'And I, for my part, do not like to be spoken to by one who does not even know who are his true father and his true mother.'

For a moment, Angus did nothing. He stood there, facing the boy, surrounded by the silence of the other players, who had heard the remark. Nobody spoke. They knew Angus was a god, but now they wondered whether he was the god they had believed him to be.

Angus turned away from his companions. Without a word to anybody, he stormed off the field and made his way back to the house of his father, Midir, who was working in a small shed, fashioning a spear from hardened wood.

'Who is my true father?' asked Angus. 'It's not you, is it?'

Midir put down the spear and turned to face the boy. He loved Angus as his own son, but he could not answer untruthfully to the boy now that he had been asked a direct question. He had long dreaded the day that Angus would find out the truth.

'No, I am not your father,' he said gently. 'I would have liked to be your father, but I am not. Your father is the god Dagda.'

Angus had heard of Dagda, as everybody had. But he was not sure that he wished to be his son.

'I am not his son,' he said to Midir.

'You are,' said Midir. 'I would not lie to you.'

'Then I must find him,' said Angus. 'I must claim what is mine.'

Midir nodded. He had often thought of how he might advise Angus when this moment came, and now was the time to explain the plan that he had made. He would tell Angus how to trick Dagda out of his kingdom and claim it back. It would be fun, he thought. Dagda had had it coming to him for some time. It would be fun – even if Dagda was his own father too.

★   ★   ★

Angus went to Dagda's place, a great mound, and was seen by Dagda's men as he approached. They ran to Dagda and said, 'Your son, Angus, has come back. He is here.' Dagda had not expected this. He was keen to see the boy after all these years, but he did not want him to stay, and even as he went down the steps of his hall to meet him he was already thinking of schemes to get Angus to go off on long journeys. He would make up a complicated quest for him, he thought – a quest which would take him off to the lands in the south, far away.

Angus stood at the bottom of the steps, awaiting his father. Then, suddenly, Dagda was there, and Angus was gazing upon his father for the first time since his infancy. He did not see himself.

'I am your son,' he said.

'So you are,' said Dagda. 'You are welcome in this house. Oh yes. Yes.'

Angus went with his father into the hall. There were many people and small gods standing around there, craning their necks to get a good view of the boy who could be their king one day if Dagda were ever to die. But Dagda was immortal, and this was not possible.

'This is a beautiful hall,' said Angus as he looked about him.

'Oh yes,' said Dagda.

'And there are many people,' Angus went on.

'Yes,' said Dagda.

Angus looked at his father. He had hoped that there might be some sign of affection, but there was none. All that he saw was a god who looked off into the distance and replied *yes* to anything that was said to him. He looked at the people and the small gods, and they looked back at him. Their eyes were bright – dark and bright – and they watched him without blinking.

Angus turned to his father. He had been told by Midir what to say to Dagda and now he addressed the god with the words that he had been given. 'Since I am your son,' Angus began.

'Oh yes,' said Dagda.

'Since I am your son,' he continued, 'you will surely let me take over your kingdom.'

Dagda was about to say *oh yes*, but he stopped himself in time and shook his head. 'That is impossible,' he said. 'I am the one. That is me. Only me.'

Angus smiled, and as he smiled there came the sound of birdsong from outside the hall. All the people and the small gods looked up sharply and gazed out of the window, hoping to see the birds who were singing in this beautiful way; but they saw nothing, in spite of their bright eyes.

'I only wish to have this place for night and day,' said Angus.

Dagda looked at him. He had heard *a night and day* and he saw no reason why he should not allow that. Then, when the boy had had his chance to be ruler for such a short time he could be dispatched on a long errand and would probably never return.

Dagda nodded. 'Yes,' he said. 'Oh yes.'

During the brief period that Angus was to be in charge, Dagda decided to go off and steal some cattle. It would be a chance to get away from his responsibilities, and he now found himself looking forward to the outing.

'Goodbye father,' said Angus, waving to Dagda from the steps of the house.

'I shall be back tomorrow,' said Dagda. 'Do not forget that. Oh yes.'

Angus smiled. He then turned to the people and small gods and told them that when the sun set that evening there would be a fine dance in the house. There would be music and a great deal of food. Everybody was pleased with this, as they did not have many dances when Dagda was in charge. In fact, they had none.

That night the musicians played all through the hours of darkness, right up until dawn, when they reluctantly put away their instruments and everybody dropped off to sleep more or less where they were standing, small gods muddled up with ordinary people, all in a sleep of exhaustion and happiness. And as they slept, Angus went round the room, stopping here and there, leaving a dream with this one and with that one, generous in his dispensing.

★　★　★

They had woken up by the time Dagda came back that afternoon. He strode up to the house and entered the hall, to find everybody rubbing their eyes and talking to one another about the fine sleep and the memorable dreams they had had. Dagda did not like parties and he ordered everybody out of the hall on pain of being smitten by his large club. But the people did nothing; they simply looked at Angus, who was sitting in a large chair normally occupied by Dagda.

'No,' said Angus. 'Nobody need leave. For I am now in charge of this place.'

Dagda looked at him, and frowned. 'You are mistaken,' he said. 'Oh yes, you are very mistaken. You were in charge only for a day and night. That is what I agreed to.'

Angus smiled sweetly. Even at a moment such as this, he bore a gentle expression. 'You agreed to my being in charge for day and night,' he corrected. 'And since night follows day and day follows night and will always do so, I am in charge forever. Is that not so?'

Angus turned to the people and small gods. And with one voice they shouted, 'Yes. Oh yes.'

And with that, the power of Dagda was broken. He moved away, shuffling out of the hall like an old man, and, cursing his son, he went off to another place, quite far away, leaving Angus in possession of everything, including his miraculous cauldron of food.

7

Another boy finds out that his father is not his father

The woman with red hair – the woman called Ginger – said, 'If you look out of this window, this one over here, where I'm standing, you can see the tip of the Whithorn Peninsula. Can you see it? There? Over there?'

The boy walked across the room to stand beside his mother. There was sunlight, and a sky that stretched up and up, emptiness into emptiness, into almost white – not that he was interested; a sky does not move everyone. He looked in the direction in which she was pointing. He moved slowly, reluctantly, and everything about him said: I don't want to do this.

'There?'

'Yes,' she said. 'That strip of blue land. That's it. See?' She was strongly aware of him beside her, a rough, pent-up masculine presence, like a wound spring, she thought. Were all fifteen-year-olds like this, she wondered; were they all as bad as this, acting as if they wanted to get rid of you, to get you out? And what exactly was required of a parent? Patience? Indifference to hostility? An anaesthesia of the feelings that would see one through to the age when they emerged from this awful chrysalis of confusion and awkwardness?

Motherhood was such a strange experience. She remembered very clearly the love that she had felt for him as a small boy, that odd little creature whom she had nurtured and protected; it had seemed to her then that she would never want anything more than to be his mother, to perform the duties that went with that. She would have died for him then, willingly, without question, but then, suddenly, he had cast off this vulnerable boyhood and become something quite different – not a man, but almost. It had happened almost overnight; she had seen a coarsening of feature, the need to shave – though not very often – heard the wild fluctuations in the voice, comical almost, but deadly serious to him, it seemed; an agony, she thought. And then, in a terrible moment one evening, when she had been bruised by some little occasion of thoughtlessness, she had found herself thinking, *I don't actually like him any more. My own son; I don't like him.*

He was their only child, born four years after the marriage. She had married at thirty, and Hal, her husband, had been forty. So now Hal was going into his late-fifties as the father of a teenage boy, while many of his contemporaries had put all that comfortably behind them. They had lived in Edinburgh to begin with, but shortly after they married they had gone to live in the Bahamas. Hal was well-off, the owner of a factory somewhere, a place that made machine tools, and the beneficiary, too, of a complicated series of trusts. The trust money had all come from shipping, he said; if one traced it far enough back it had come from large ships that plied routes between India and Europe. There was jute there too, somewhere in the background; one of those Scottish jute fortunes. There was so much.

In the Bahamas they acquired a house over-looking a cove; a house with shady verandahs in the Caribbean style and lawns. There was a gazebo where one could sit to benefit from the breezes that touched that higher point of land. There were parties, with steel bands, and waiters in white gloves moving among the guests, and high night skies above, in which the constellations seemed like suspended lights set out for the party below. There was a tennis player who came to these parties. He was American and had helped to coach tennis at a private university in Tennessee before something happened and he had been obliged to leave. It had been something sexual, but nobody knew what it was. The coach played with her on Wednesday and Friday, and Hal watched them from the house. He did not like to play with a strong player like that, as his serve was weak and he felt ashamed of it, of everything really.

She had a troublesome pregnancy and was often weepy. When he eventually arrived, Mark was brought into the world by a tall Jamaican doctor with large hands and a pencil-thin moustache. She said that he always looked sad, this doctor, even when he delivered a baby. The nurse who came with him smiled. She said, 'Jesus has given you a son, Mrs McNair. You give thanks to Jesus.' The doctor said nothing, and did not smile.

'Forgive me for saying this,' she said to him once, after a check-up. 'Forgive me for saying this, Dr Roy, but you always look so sad. Maybe I shouldn't ask, but why is that?'

He had been washing his hands, his back turned to her. There was a powerful smell of strong soap. And cloves somewhere; there was oil of cloves.

'I have a sad job,' he said, still turned away from her. 'Doctoring is a sad job, you know.'

She buttoned her blouse. 'All the time? Surely not all the time.'

'People are dying all the time,' he muttered. 'All of us. We're all dying, Mrs McNair. Rich people dying. Poor people dying. Everyone.'

She had burst out laughing. 'That's an odd view to take of life! Why, if we all thought that, we'd give up, wouldn't we? There'd be no point in going on.'

He turned off the taps and reached for a towel. He said nothing, but reached for his prescription pad and scribbled something on it. He gave her the piece of paper, staring at her with his sad eyes. She wondered whether he did not like her because she was white; whether he had not forgiven the injustice, but remembered it, saw it still, and bore witness to it. *We're all dying. Rich people, poor people . . . but not at the same rate. The poor died much more.*

Of course there was everything laid on for the baby when he arrived. There was a nurse, a Honduran woman who had managed to get to the island and had found a husband and a job. The husband cut the hedges in people's gardens, travelling around the island in an old pick-up truck which bore the legend *Eddie's Hedge Fund*. 'That's very funny,' Ginger said to the nurse. But the nurse had looked at her blankly and said, 'Not funny. It's very hard work. Eddie works all the time. Clip clip.'

She did not have much to do, and having the

nurse at hand meant that even the routine tasks of looking after the baby were lightened. She went to bridge parties twice a week, where they talked about the same things week-in, week-out. There were little scandals and big; nothing on the island seemed private for long, except for the real secrets, the big ones, which people kept to themselves, away from prying eyes.

Her husband kept an office at the back of the house. This was where he managed his affairs, spending hours on the telephone to the managers who ran the machine tool company, irritating them, she suspected. And apart from that he worked on his boat, a sleek thirty-two-foot yacht that was moored in the cove below the house. There were always things to strip down and varnish, and it kept him reasonably busy. She did not like this boat, because she suffered from seasickness. Even the mildest of swells would send her to the side, nauseous, retching.

His interest in the boat, and her lack of interest in it, reflected the divide between them, the absence of common ground. They read different things: he was fascinated by naval history, and would pore over books which she found unreadable, while she devoured novels, books he described as pointless, puzzling; she liked to listen to music which grated on his ear – big bands, dance bands – while his taste ran to Italian tenors.

She felt bored, even trapped, but she stuck to the marriage because she depended on him. She liked luxury; she liked not having to worry about money, and, most of all, she could not face the prospect of having to work for a living. She knew people whose divorce settlements were perfectly adequate – there were some of them on the island – but could one trust the courts? What if the judge took a poor view of women who left their husbands? Women stuck together, and why should one not expect men to do the same and to use their power to favour their own? There were women judges, of course, but were there any on the island? She thought not. If she had heard of generous divisions of property, she had heard equally of divisions that were far from that. And she knew that she could not tolerate a fall from where she was. That was out of the question. She would die if that happened.

When Mark was eight they decided to send him off the island for schooling.

'He can go back to Scotland,' Hal said. 'I want him to get a Scottish education. There's a place in Perthshire. A little boarding school. He can go there.'

He said that, but it took him a long time to do so, as he stuttered badly. Sometimes it would be a minute or two before he overcame a block, and the words then came tumbling out until he reached the next stumbling point. She was used to it, but it was embarrassing for those who were not. Some of them did not know where to look; others tried to help him by suggesting words, but that only made matters worse.

It was a wrench seeing Mark off to school. She travelled with him to Scotland and put him in the boarding school. He was excited, but she was sure that he would feel homesick after the novelty had worn off. 'So many of them do,' said the matron. 'Particularly when the parents live so far away.'

'Oh . . .'

'But they get over it,' continued the matron. 'Little boys are tough. They can get by without us adults, you know. They can get by quite well.'

'I suppose they did in *Lord of the Flies*,' she said. 'Although . . .'

The matron looked at her without comprehension. 'Flies?'

'A book. A group of boys were stranded on an island. They reverted to savagery.'

The matron lit a cigarette. Ginger noticed that her fingers were stained with nicotine. 'Little savages. Yes. They can be.'

He came back for school holidays. It sometimes seemed to her as if he was more distant, as if he needed her less, but that was only sometimes; on other occasions, particularly when he was due to be sent back to school, he would be a little boy again, holding on to her, clingy.

'I'm not happy sending him back,' she said to her husband. 'I really don't like it. Couldn't we go back ourselves . . .'

The suggestion seemed to horrify him. He struggled to get the words out. His face flushed red. Small specks of released spittle accompanied each sentence. 'We can't possibly. We can't. Think of the money we would have to give over to the taxman. Do you realise how much it would be each year?' It had taken him so long to say this that he reached for a pad of paper, scribbled down a figure, and passed it to her. The figure had been followed by three exclamation marks.

She shrugged. There seemed to her to be little point in tax exile if one was unhappy. And there was surely enough money not to notice the difference of . . . she glanced at the figure again — it was almost six hundred thousand pounds. Would he miss six hundred thousand pounds a year? She doubted it.

But, as the years passed, she became progressively more bored in the Bahamas. And rather to her surprise, he did too, although at first he was careful not to show it. It was a matter of pride, really; it had been his idea to go there in the first place and their departure would be an admission that it had not been the right choice. He was sensitive, and did not like to be bettered in an argument or shown to be wrong. He was possessive too, jealous of what was his.

Once they had made the decision to move, they quickly found a house in the south-west of Scotland.

'You're almost in Ireland down there,' he said. 'In fact, from parts you can see Ireland on a clear day.'

She spoke to somebody who said that the weather would be good. 'It's warmer,' they said. 'If you have to live in Scotland, then that's the place to be.'

Shortly after they had bought the house – a large house, with two wings and a gatehouse – they drove up to Perthshire to see Mark, now fourteen, at his boarding school – a bigger school now – tucked away in a quiet glen. It was an afternoon set aside for visits by parents, with sporting events and, in the evening, a play put on by the members of the school's drama club.

Mark was taciturn. He looked about him before he spoke, and she wondered whether he was being bullied. It was almost as if he was afraid of somebody coming up to him and forcibly contradicting him: the little that he said was almost whispered. But then she realised that it was embarrassment, and that he did not want the other boys to see them. That was not unusual, of course; teenagers were often embarrassed by their parents and tried to avoid being seen with them, but even if it was normal, it was still hurtful.

She felt like grabbing him, shaking him, and demanding, 'What exactly do you think is wrong with us?' but she stopped herself. It would not have helped, she thought, and anyway she knew what was wrong. It was his father's stuttering. He did not want any of his schoolfellows to hear him.

She bit her tongue. His father was a generous man. He provided for them without complaint. He paid for this expensive school; he paid for everything. If they did not have him, they would be paupers: she had nothing of her own.

'Be kind to your father,' she whispered to him, shortly before they left.

He glowered at her indignantly. 'What?' he hissed. 'What?'

'I said, be kind to your father. Just be kind. That's all.'

'I am.'

'You aren't,' she whispered back. 'You aren't.'

He looked about him to see if anybody was witnessing this. 'You're always getting at me,' he said between clenched teeth. 'You sent me away. You wanted to get rid of me.'

She could not reply to this, as her husband had come up to them. He smiled at his son and tried to say something, but the stutter came on, and there were no words. The boy looked away while his father tried to speak.

Later, when the parents had all disappeared, and the life of the school returned to normal, his friend, the boy who lived in the compartment next to him in the boarding house said to him, 'That was your father? That man with your mother? That was him?'

He looked down at the floor. He nodded.

'Doesn't look like you,' said his friend. 'I would never have guessed. No, really – I wouldn't have. Not ever. He looks different, you know. No offence. He just looks different.'

There was silence. He glanced up at his friend, searching his face for the spirit of the remark; there was no guile.

'People can look very different from their parents,' Mark said. 'There's no reason why you have to look the same.'

The other boy nodded. 'Yes, sure. Sure. But you know you get your eyes from your parents. Your eyes are blue, aren't they? Sort of blue. But they both have brown eyes, don't they? Maybe I didn't see properly, but I think that they were brown.'

He shrugged. 'Not always. It's not always like that.'

The other boy lost interest. Something was happening at the other end of the room, an argument about something, and his attention had been diverted. But Mark stood there for a few minutes, thinking. The idea that the man who claimed to be his father was not his real father did not displease him. In fact, that night it kept him awake with its possibilities. It was not that he wanted to discover who his true father was – he found that rather uninteresting, although his true father, whoever he was, would not be like that; what intrigued him was the thought that the man whom he had come to despise was nothing to do with him. That was an exciting thought.

A month later he came home for the holidays. This was the first time that he had been in the new house, and she took pleasure in showing him round. And now they were standing at the window looking at the Whithorn peninsula in the distance. Her husband was away for a few days, in London, where there was business to attend to.

'That's where the saints came to Scotland,' she said. 'St Ninian lived down there.'

He looked away. He did not care about St Ninian.

'I'm sure that you're going to like this house,' she said.

'I liked the Bahamas.'

She bit her lip. 'Well, so did I,' she said. 'But I like Scotland too.'

He said nothing, and after a few moments she started to move away. 'You should go and have a look at the loch. Daddy says there are some lovely trout in it. It's been well stocked. You could use his rod . . .'

He spun round. 'He's not my real father. I know he isn't.'

She was quite still. Her voice was barely audible, a whisper really. 'What did you say?'

He looked hot and awkward. 'I said, he's not my real father. I've found out.'

She took a deep breath. Her heart was pounding within her, and she heard the shrill sound of her tinnitus. It always happened when she became stressed, when her blood pressure went up. It was like the sound of a forest of distant cicadas.

'But of course he's your father. Where on earth did you get the idea? I've never heard such nonsense.' She wondered whether she sounded convincing enough.

The boy raised a hand, as if he was about to make some gesture, but dropped it. 'There's a place you can send samples too. It's in Australia. I saw it on the web. It doesn't cost much. I sent his comb. It was in the car when you came to the school. I sent that and some hairs of mine.'

She stared at him wide-eyed. She did not know that this was a lie – that he had not sent anything away; she did not know that this was his way of testing her for the truth of what he suspected.

She sat down. She wanted to run from the room, to get away, but she sat down. He looked at her, accusing, waiting for her to say something.

'I suppose I should tell you,' she said at last. 'I didn't want to. I never wanted to.'

It seemed that he was as shocked as she was. His voice was unsteady. 'Who's my father then?'

'He was a very nice man,' she said quietly. 'He

taught me tennis. We became very good friends. I'm so sorry about it. I know that what I did was unfair to your father . . . to Daddy. And I'm not sure if you'll understand.'

'I don't care,' he said. 'But I'm going to tell him that I'm not his son. I want him to know.'

She rose to her feet and reached out for him, wildly. 'You mustn't! You mustn't tell Daddy! That's the one thing you mustn't, mustn't do! Please, Mark! Please!'

He wrenched himself away from her. He felt elated now; this gave him power. He could pay them both back now. For leaving the Bahamas. For embarrassing him. For being so different from him. For everything.

She tried to talk to him later that day, once she had marshalled her thoughts. But he turned his back on her and walked out of the room, and she did not feel up to chasing after him. Of course it would still be several days before Hal came back, and she could work on him during that time, but she had to accept, she thought, that he might just go ahead and tell Hal. And if he did that, then there was no telling how Hal would react, although she feared that it would be badly. Hal was jealous, and the knowledge that she had had an affair and passed off the result as his own son could goad him into something terrible – leaving her, in particular. That would mean giving all this up – this new house, the security, everything. She was staring at poverty; poverty and the need to work.

She decided that she would have to talk to somebody about it, and she telephoned her brother, who lived in Glasgow. She asked him to drive down and visit her that day, and he agreed: he could tell that there was something wrong and he had always been supportive.

'Where's Mark?' he asked, when he arrived. 'I haven't seen him for ages.'

She waved a hand vaguely in the direction of the outside. 'Somewhere,' she said. 'Actually, it's him I want to talk to you about.'

Her brother frowned. 'Teenage behaviour?'

She sighed. 'Can you stay here tonight? Hal's away.'

'I had assumed you would want me to stay, Ginger,' he said. 'Annie's not expecting me back.'

'Good. Come into the kitchen.'

She poured a handful of coffee beans into a grinder. 'I may as well be direct,' she said. 'I'm no angel. A long time ago I had an affair. It was in the Bahamas.'

He looked at her. She had not been expecting him to be disapproving, and he was not. He had had an affair too, several, in fact, but he was not intending to tell her about them.

'And now he's turned up?'

She looked at him blankly, and he spoke again. 'The man in question. Your friend. He's reappeared?'

'No. Nothing like that.' She paused, and looked at her brother. He was a tall man, fair-haired. His eyes were kind, and she loved him a great deal. She used to call him Mr Loopy when they were small, and she still thought of him as that, though she did not use the name. Now she thought: *I can confess to him. I can confess to him because he is my brother.*

'Mark is that man's son,' she said evenly. 'Now he's discovered this, and he's going to tell Hal. I've tried reasoning with him, I've begged him, but he's got the bit between his teeth. You know what he's like. He's going to tell him.'

He looked at her, and reached out to touch her lightly on the arm. 'He can't. Hal will . . .'

'Yes,' she said. 'He could do anything.' She was silent for a moment, and then she said, 'I shouldn't have done it. I was bored. I don't know what came over me . . . And it was a long time ago, you know. Fifteen years.'

She looked at him. Mr Loopy.

'I try to be a good wife for Hal. I do my best. I don't want to hurt him.'

'No. Of course not.'

She made a gesture of helplessness. 'And yet Mark seems dead-set on doing just that.'

Her brother kept his hand on her arm. 'I suspect he is. This father and son business is not always simple. Freud . . . Well, Freud.' He paused, looking at her quizzically. 'Do you want me to do something?'

She was weeping now, quietly. She nodded her head. 'If you could try. But I don't see what . . .'

He was thinking. 'If persuasion hasn't worked,' he muttered.

'It hasn't,' she said quickly. 'It hasn't.'

'I'll try,' he said. 'I'll have a word with him.'

She looked at him gratefully, although she thought that it was unlikely that he would succeed where she had failed.

They had dinner together, the three of them, sitting awkwardly at the dining-room table. Mark said very little, not responding to any of the conversational gambits tried by his uncle. So brother and sister talked together, and the boy excused himself early from the table, saying that he was going up to his room.

'I'll come up and say goodnight later on,' her brother said as the boy walked behind his chair.

The boy looked round. 'If you want,' he muttered.
'I do want.'

Mark left the room, like an area of low pressure,
of bad weather, moving off the meteorological map.
The two of them went back into the kitchen. She
poured him a whisky and herself a glass of wine.
They raised the glasses to each other in the easy
familiarity of brother and sister; so much shared;
so much that never really needed to be said.

'Don't worry,' he said. 'You don't have to worry.'

She shook her head. 'Let's not talk about it right
now. I feel quite sick when I think of it.'

'All right,' he said, 'I won't. But I must say that
I find it very difficult to like my nephew. Sorry to
say that, but I do.' He had never liked him, but of
course he had never revealed his feelings. Now he
had come out and said it, it seemed so easy, and so
natural.

She was silent for a moment, looking at him, and
he thought that he had overstepped the mark —
there were limits to honesty and the speaking of
one's mind. But then she sighed, and said, 'And I'm

afraid I have to say the same thing. Oh my God, isn't that awful? For a mother to say that? Don't you think that's awful, Angus?'

He tried to reassure her. He had no children of his own, but he understood the loyalty of parents. 'Some children make it difficult. But then they change. They grow up. They change.'

He wondered. What if he said to her, let's get rid of him. Let's have an accident on the loch. A boat that capsized and the boy unfortunately knocked his head on the side. How would she react? He could not say that, of course, because people like them did not do that sort of thing. But it was tempting.

He looked at his watch. It was almost ten o'clock.

'I'm going upstairs,' he said. 'I'm tired.'

She rose to her feet and planted a kiss on his cheek. 'Thank you so much for coming down here, Angus. Just having you here is a help. It makes me feel safer. It really does.'

'I'm your brother,' he said. He felt awkward with signs, and words, of affection, but he knew that she understood him and would know how he felt.

He went upstairs. She had told him that his bedroom was at the end of the corridor, next to Mark's.

He saw that there was no light coming from
under Mark's door. So the boy had turned off his
light and gone to sleep. He pushed at the door and
a square of light fell onto the bedroom floor. On
the other side of the room, he could make out the
boy's form under the blankets and the head on the
pillow. He crossed the floor silently until he was
standing at the head of the bed, his shadow falling
upon the boy's face. He bent down, so that his head
was right next to the boy's.

'Mark,' he whispered. 'This is your Uncle Angus.
Stay quite still now. Don't move at all. Just listen
to me.'

The boy stirred slightly. The eyelids, he saw, were
slightly open, flickering. He murmured something
drowsily.

'Good. Now listen very carefully. Here's a little
bedtime story for you. The story of the little
princes in the Tower of London. Their uncle came
in and he took a pillow, just like this one.' He

reached out and picked up the spare pillow on the other side of the bed. He held it above the boy's face. 'Just like this. And he smothered them, I'm sorry to say.'

He lowered the pillow slightly. The boy's eyes had opened more now, but he was quite still.

'And then that was the end of them,' he whispered. 'A wicked uncle, don't you think? But then some uncles are like that, not all, but some. And I want you to know that if you tell your father that you are not his son, then I'd be very careful of pillows – and uncles . . . if you understand me.'

He stopped. He could hear the boy's breathing. It was short and shallow.

'I would like you to give me a sign that you have understood me,' said Angus. 'Just a little nod, that's all. Just to show that we understand one another.'

He watched. The boy's head moved slightly on the pillow. Up and down.

8

Angus is kind to pigs

There were people who had been changed into pigs, something which happened from time to time in those days. They lived in a part of Ireland where there were many places for pigs to find food; where there were nuts that grew in profusion on low branches that pigs could reach; where there were small ditches rich in the most succulent and delicious pig food. These pigs had a village that they had made, a small village of round houses with turf roofs, and they lived in this village, rising early in the morning to feel the sun on their backs and the dew underfoot. They were contented enough.

The happiness of these pigs was interrupted by the arrival of hunting hounds. The pigs were strong warriors, able to protect themselves against most threats, but they did not like having to keep watch all the time for lurking hounds. A shadow could be a shadow, or it could be a hound. A howling sound could be the sound of the wind across the stones, or it could come from the throat of a hound. The pigs could not tolerate such uncertainty, such fear. They moved from their village, leaving behind the houses they had made, leaving the abundant nuts, the well-worn paths through their village, all their memories. From the top of a nearby hill, people watched the pigs run behind their leader, a stream of excited squealing, a river of bristle; and then there was just the sound of birdsong and the rustling of the leaves like dice.

The pigs came to Angus, and he received them. He allowed them to press their moist snouts against his toes and his ankles; he allowed them to gaze at the birds that flew around his head. They could stay with him, he said, living down at the bottom of a field near his house. They inspected this place and declared themselves satisfied. The mother of the pigs looked up at Angus, and there was gratitude in her tiny, dark eyes. And there was light in these eyes, too; the light of intelligence.

Angus heard the pigs singing. He would stand on a small hillock and listen to the sound of the pigs' songs carried upon the breeze. Some of these songs were for the weddings of pigs, and they were sweet songs, full of love. Others were sad songs, for the funeral of a pig, who would be carried on the backs of its brothers and sisters and laid in a place where the pigs would normally not venture.

But there were people who ate these pigs, although the pigs were really people turned into pigs. How were such people to know? And so they fell upon these pigs, turning them upside down and cutting their throats so that the pig blood was red and bright in the sun. When this happened the other pigs sang their sad songs for the one that had gone and their words were full of regret for the fact that they had been changed into pigs.

The pigs could not bear such losses, and such insult. They were reluctant to leave Angus, but it was not possible for them to stay. They gathered in a great meeting of pigs and moved slowly across

the hillside and away to another part of the country.
Angus saw them go, watching the small flags of the
pigs fluttering in the breeze.

9

Is there a place for pigs there?

Pig Twenty, a male, donor of magic skin, was the son of Pig Nineteen, a large, lazy sow whose sole interest was food. With her small porcine eyes – cunning eyes, said some of the scientists – Pig Nineteen looked out at a world which she divided into edible and non-edible. The non-edible was of no interest to her, but she engaged with the edible passionately, sniffing it out with her moist, mucus-encrusted nose, scrabbling for it with her cloven feet, and gobbling it down with a grunting that could have been triumph, contentment or sorrow at the realisation that food was finite.

By virtue of the nature of his conception, a miraculous one, Pig Twenty had no siblings. His life had begun in a glass dish in a laboratory near Glasgow, a laboratory called, quite simply, the Research Centre, and it was there, in a world of gleaming surfaces and bright lights, that the human and the porcine were brought together. If there is any glory in human genetic material, then a bit of that, even if only a few sequences of DNA, was fused into the architecture of Pig Twenty's cells; not enough to make him anything but a pig, but enough to endow some of his organs, particularly his skin, with a friendliness to human cells. And this, in due course, meant that Pig Twenty and his offspring could donate tissue to human beings in need. It was not a donation of which they would have any inkling, but it would at least be the cause of human gratitude, somewhere.

Pig Twenty lived in an enclosure made of concrete. At one end of it there was a small brick shelter with a slatted wooden floor. At the other end was a trough into which his food would be poured and a small indentation in the concrete floor which served as a pool of sorts. Pig Twenty was encouraged to bathe in this, but he rarely did so. The water seemed to make him uncomfortable, his keeper said. It was almost as if it made him itchy.

IS THERE A PLACE FOR PIGS THERE?

Pig Twenty could see the sky if he looked up
– a rectangle of blue or grey above the enclosure;
a place of birds and the movement of clouds,
which sometimes caught his attention, but only
momentarily. Because of the concrete walls he
could see nothing of the world beyond; not the
fenced area where the scientists parked their cars,
not the low-lying buildings which housed the lab-
oratories, not the line of trees to the side of those
buildings and the hills beyond. None of these things
came into the narrow universe of Pig Twenty.

His days were dull. He slept in the shed, or sometimes on a pile of straw near the enclosure gate. He
looked at the ground, as if trying to find something
there, and failing to see it. He scratched himself,
rather too much said the vet who examined him
from time to time, and who rubbed a thick white
cream into inflamed portions of his skin. And sometimes he just stood, waiting by the gate for something to happen and then retreating to the shed
when it did not.

Pig Twenty was looked after by a young man

who acted as keeper for the twenty or so pigs belonging to the Research Centre, and for the large number of rats which were kept for experimental use. This young man had worked there since he left school at the age of sixteen. He was now twenty-four, and it was assumed by everyone at the Centre that he would be there for as long as the Centre survived. 'He has no ambition, that laddie,' said one of the older secretaries, as she gazed out of the window at the keeper outside. 'Just look at him. He often just stands, you know. Just stands there. Goodness knows what goes on in that head of his.'

The other secretary, a young woman with frizzy hair, looked. She saw the keeper standing outside Pig Twenty's enclosure, a brush in his hand. 'Pretty head, though,' she said. 'But he seems to like the pigs. If you like pigs, then it must be a good enough job.'

'I hate pigs. Hate their pinkness.'

'That's you. Not everyone's the same, you know. He doesn't. But still, it must be odd to have no ambition, not to want to be something more. I can't imagine he's well paid.'

'He isn't. I've seen the payroll. He gets less than anybody else. He's on some sort of odd agricultural scale, and he's at the bottom of it.'

He did not need much money, though. He lived with his parents in a cottage on the edge of the nearby village, a short walk away if one crossed the fields rather than walking along the main road. Their house was one of a short row of miners' cottages, built when the coalfields under that rich bit of earth were in full production. The cottages had that look of housing that is built by the rich for the poor to live in: solidly enough constructed so that they should last for generations of workers, but small, because such people were thought to have modest needs – a bedroom for the parents and one for all the children, a living room which doubled up as a kitchen, a tiny bathroom at the back. That was all.

The mines closed down in a bitter clash of ideologies and brute economics; Colombian coal was

cheap and Scottish was expensive. The keeper's
father was paid off, which was no great disaster for
him as he had almost reached retirement age and
his lungs would not have stood much more of the
colliery air. He started to breed pigeons in the back
garden, using their droppings to fertilise the neat
rows of vegetables he planted each spring. He went
to the pub in the village in the early evening and
sat there, eking out his glass of beer, talking to
other ex-miners. Then he went home, checked up
on the pigeons, and ate the supper that his wife
would prepare for him and his son. It was always
the same thing – mince and potatoes with green
beans or peas from a can. At weekends they ate a
piece of lamb or beef. There was plenty of meat,
because he had known what it was like to have no
meat for the table and he was determined that his
family should not experience that lack. On occasion
his son, the keeper, brought home a pig that had
died at the Centre – although this was against the
rules – and the two of them would slice it up in
the back garden, watched by the cooing pigeons,

and dispose of the innards and the head by burning them in a small pit which he used for bonfires. Then they would eat pork for the next couple of weeks, giving some to the neighbours in gratitude for their forbearance over the smoke from the pit and the constant sound of the pigeons.

'I like pork,' said the woman next door. 'I really like it. I can never have enough pork. That's not a hint, of course – it's just what I feel.'

The keeper was an unusual young man. He had been dreamy at school, frustrating his teachers. They saw ability in him, but they could not get him to use it. He just seemed to be happy with how he was and where he was, and any suggestion that he might better himself was met with a blank smile.

'You could do really well, you know,' said the mathematics teacher. 'You've got a good head on your shoulders, you know that? You're not stupid. But you won't work. You won't work.'

He smiled, but said nothing.

'A boy like you could take advantage of these

schemes the universities have these days. You don't have to be well-off to go to university, you know. Not these days. You could do it. You could. But it won't happen by magic. Nothing happens by magic. Nothing.'

Again he smiled. 'I don't think I want to go to university. I'm fine here.'

The teacher looked through the window, beyond the fence around the school, across the road to the rolling hills. He could not make out this boy, try as he might; he could not understand him. He was happy enough, as far as he could tell, and the parents seemed all right – nothing special, but a decent couple. Perhaps that was the trouble. If one was unhappy at home one might want to get away, to do something different, but if one was contented then one might be inclined to stay.

'So you wouldn't like to be a doctor? Something like that?'

'No.'

'What would you want to be then?'

'Something.'

'That's no answer.'

When he left school, that same teacher said to him, 'You're an odd one, you know. But you know what? I reckon you're happier than all the others. You really are. And this job you've got yourself – that job at the Centre, I suspect you'll do that very well.'

And the boy had looked at him and shaken his hand. 'Thank you, sir. Thank you for everything you've taught me.'

It was the first time that a pupil had said that to that teacher, and he turned away so that the emotion he felt should not be seen.

His work at the Research Centre was undemanding. He cleaned the cages occupied by the rats and the pig enclosures. He fed the animals too, and was responsible for taking them to the lab. He collected the bodies of the rats after the experiments were completed and placed them in the small incinerator which it was his duty to fire up and clean. He did not like this duty and he hung his head as he did it, as if he were participating in something wrong. The Director saw this once, from his window, and called him up to his office.

'I noticed you down there looking a bit downcast,' he said. 'That can't be the most pleasant job here. But if you feel that you want to talk to me about it, then you must do so. We could talk about the good things that we achieve here. You know about those, don't you?'

He nodded. 'The rats are dead when I burn them,' he said. 'They don't feel. You don't feel when you're dead.'

The Director looked at him over his desk. Odd, he thought. Very odd. But that's what some of these people are like. The people from those villages. Not very . . . well, they were just a bit on the *gleikit* side. He thought of the Scots word which summed it up so expressively. *Gleikit* – not quite all there; one sandwich short of the full picnic. So expressive.

Later, the Director said to the secretary with the frizzy hair, 'I talked to the animal keeper this morning. You know, that young man who cleans the cages. Odd. He's a bit odd. Always smiles. But odd.'

'I know,' said the secretary. 'But I hear he does his job very well. Nobody complains, do they?'

'Certainly not.' The Director thought for a moment. 'But what makes him tick?'

'Good question,' said the secretary. She paused. Then: 'But, as you know, the people round here . . . well.'

The Director smiled. 'Yes, but we don't say that, do we?' He put a finger to his lips, indicating silence, and the secretary with the frizzy hair laughed. The Director looked at her.

Later that day, when she was just about to leave the Centre after work, the secretary walked past the keeper. He was coming from the pig enclosures, wiping his hands on a piece of old cloth. She greeted him, and he smiled back at her. But he did not speak. She went home and thought no more of the encounter. But the next morning, when she awoke she remembered that she had experienced an unsettling dream. It was not an unpleasant dream – just unsettling. She had dreamed of the keeper.

She got out of bed and made herself a cup of

coffee. Standing in front of her window, she looked down at the small garden behind her house and watched the sun touch the leaves of the shrubs she had planted the year before. She found herself smiling as she recalled the events of the dream. It had been so improbable, as dreams so often are, and she wondered whether she would think of this when she next saw him; how could she not smile, not give herself away, if she did? And she thought of him again on her way to work, when she turned off the road to the Centre and saw in the distance the roofs of the cottages where she had been told that he lived. What was there for a young man to do there, she wondered? What sense of future could there be in a place like that?

A few days later the Director and two of the scientists asked the keeper to bring Pig Twenty to the lab. He loaded him on to the small trolley that he used for moving pigs about; it was no use trying to lead a pig on a piece of rope; they were always tugging in the wrong direction, panicking at the unfamiliar smell of the lab, squealing, trying to run off to a freedom that they had never seen, but which they somehow sensed.

Pig Twenty was silent. He was familiar with the keeper, who had a way with animals – a way of calming them – and he co-operated as the keeper pushed him onto the ramp which led up into the trolley. He looked up at the sky, which had suddenly become larger for him, and he stared at nearby objects – a box, a bale of straw, the keeper's legs. This was the world, suddenly expanded.

Within a few minutes the keeper had him in the laboratory, standing on a small platform, restrained on either side by a stainless-steel bar. Pig Twenty shivered. He looked up at the keeper, who was standing to his side, a hand resting on his skin. Pig Twenty could feel the pressure. He felt the human fingers on his hide. He itched.

One of the scientists put a needle into his side and drew off a small quantity of blood. The keeper watched as the tube of the cylinder filled with pig blood.

'They make black puddings out of that,' the keeper said to the scientist.

The scientist glanced up at him. Strange boy, he thought. 'Not here,' he said. 'Not here. Can't stand black pudding, anyway. Pork chops, yes. But black pudding – no. Cooked blood, for heaven's sake.'

'Bacon sandwiches for me,' said the other scientist. 'Not the most sophisticated thing in the world, but pretty delicious.'

'Chokes your arteries,' said the other scientist, squirting the blood out of the syringe into a small phial.

The keeper looked at Pig Twenty. He reached out and touched the animal on the snout, which seemed to reassure him. The pale pink skin was soft to the touch, moist, warm.

'Starve him tomorrow,' said the first scientist. 'Water's all right, but no food.'

The keeper looked surprised. 'Why?'

'We're harvesting tissue on Thursday. And he'll be on antibiotics until then. I'll give him the first dose now, and somebody will come and administer more tomorrow and the day afterwards. Understand?'

The keeper looked away. They were going to kill Pig Twenty. He wheeled him back to his enclosure and opened the gate. Pig Twenty, smelling his familiar surroundings, dashed forward down the ramp, slipping as he did so. He tumbled, fell to his knees, and grunted involuntarily. The keeper reached forward and helped him up. Unsteadily, Pig Twenty moved forward and re-entered his quarters.

That evening, on the way home, walking across the fields, the keeper thought about Pig Twenty. He knew that harvesting tissue was what the Centre did – it happened all the time – but he had become fond of Pig Twenty, in spite of what he had been told by his predecessor in the job. He had said, 'Don't get attached to the animals. Just don't. Animals die. That's why they're here.' Like miners, thought the keeper; they died after they had been underground too long. We still have coal, so people are dying, somewhere, somewhere far away, for the coal.

They ate their dinner in the kitchen, with his

father at one end of the table and his mother at the other, and him in the middle. It was the same meal that they always had: mince and potatoes, and his father said the things that he always said. He talked about his pigeons. His mother, though, said to him, 'Why don't you go to a dance some time?'

He looked at his plate. 'I don't want to. I'm happy here.'

She moved the bowl of potatoes across the table towards him. 'Eat some more potatoes,' she said. 'You don't eat enough.'

'He does,' said his father. 'He eats. Look, he's eaten everything that you put on his plate.'

'You should go to a dance,' said his mother. 'There are plenty of dances. Every night.'

'That's half the trouble,' said his father. 'All those dances. The country's drunk. Drunk. Dancing all the time.' He paused, and looked at his son. 'Leave him be. Just leave him be.'

The keeper stared down at his plate. He was thinking of Pig Twenty. He imagined him in his shelter, cold on this chilly evening; lonely too. He said, 'There's a pig that they don't want at work. I can bring him back here if I like.'

His mother nodded. 'Good. I can freeze him, or most of him.'

'Chops,' said his father. 'Lots of chops.'

'He's not dead,' said the keeper.

'Then we can slaughter him,' said his father. 'You. Me. The two of us. We can kill him out the back.'

'Not to kill,' said their son. 'I want to keep him. There's room in the shed. He can sleep there.'

The woman looked at her husband, who shrugged. 'If you want,' he said.

'And the smell?' said the woman.

'This pig keeps himself clean,' said the keeper. 'And think of the manure for the vegetables. Think of it.'

The man nodded. 'Yes. It will be good for them. You're right enough there.'

They finished their meal in silence. Then, when the dishes had been cleared away, the keeper's father went out into the back garden and gave grain to the pigeons in the small pigeon lofts he had built for them and fixed to the back wall of the house. 'My beauties,' he muttered, as the birds cooed to him, shuffling about on their tiny, spurred feet. 'Wee feathered beauties.'

While his father was attending to his birds, the keeper put on his coat and slipped out of the front door. Then, following the path across the fields, he made his way back to the Centre. He had a key to the gate around the animal houses, and he let himself in and walked over to Pig Twenty's enclosure. It was almost dark by now, but there was enough of the evening's light left for Pig Twenty to see him and to come out to greet him, nuzzling against the rough material of his trousers, lifting his snout expectantly for some titbit. The keeper reached into the pocket of his jacket and took out a long piece of green twine. He made a loop and a noose, and slipped this round Pig Twenty's neck. Pig Twenty itched and looked at the ground.

It took him almost an hour to get Pig Twenty across the fields and round the back of the small line of cottages. The pig kept stopping, digging his trotters into the ground in order to inspect something – a pile of leaves, a ditch with a trickle of water running through it, a hedge, the world. But eventually they reached the old shed in the garden and he pushed Pig Twenty into it.

'You'll be fine,' he whispered, scratching the pig's back and then pushing him onto a pile of sacking. 'Lie down there.'

The next afternoon, when the scientist came to administer the antibiotic, he found Pig Twenty's enclosure empty. He called the keeper.

'That pig. Where the hell is it?'

The keeper shrugged.

'He's not in that sty of his,' the scientist said. 'And if you don't know where he is, then he must have escaped.' The scientist looked over his shoulder, towards the fields.

'Maybe,' said the keeper.

'You'd better find him,' said the scientist. 'Don't just stand there. If he gets out and mixes with other pigs there'll be trouble. That pig is a biohazard. You realise that, do you?'

The keeper shrugged, and the scientist, angry, walked away. A few minutes later the secretary came to fetch the keeper. She looked at him and then looked away. She had dreamed of him again, and it had been more vivid this time. If only he knew, she thought, with a certain embarrassment; what would he think? She blushed.

'The Director wants you,' she said. 'Right now.'

'All right.'

She looked at him again, with concern this time. 'Are you in trouble?'

'A pig's gone,' he said.

She laughed. 'So that's all.'

He smiled now. 'They were going to kill it.'

She frowned. 'It wouldn't have known about that.'

He said nothing. She glanced at him again, and the thought occurred to her. He had taken the pig.

'What's a biohazard?' he suddenly asked.

She raised an eyebrow. 'Didn't you go to school?'

He did not answer. 'It's a danger,' she said. 'Something that's dangerous. Radiation. That sort of thing.' She paused. 'Do you know what radiation is?'

'No.'

They were walking towards the Director's office now. She stopped, and reached out to take hold of his arm. She noticed that his arm felt soft under her touch; and that is how he had been in her dream, gentle.

'You've taken that pig, haven't you?'

He nodded.

'Well, we need to get it back,' she said. 'Where is it? At your place?'

He lowered his eyes. It was as if he was ashamed. 'I don't steal things,' he muttered.

She wanted to reassure him. 'Of course you don't. Of course you don't.'

She looked about her. There was still time, she imagined, if they went now. They could bring the pig back and come up with some explanation for its absence. She could intercede on his behalf with the Director, who liked her and would, she suspected, be happy to be seen by her as understanding, as liberal.

They turned back. He led her across the fields, her shoes, unsuitable for the country, becoming lined with heavy lumps of mud that she had to stop and scrape off on clumps of grass.

'It's not normally this muddy,' he said. 'The rain . . .'

'Of course. But I'll be all right. Don't worry. It's only mud, and look, it's coming off. See?'

They skirted round the side of the cottage and into the garden at the back. She saw that there was somebody in the kitchen, a shape moving behind a window of frosted glass, a light glowing in the background. These cottages needed to have their lights switched on during the daytime, she thought, because the windows were so mean. There was a smell coming from the house, the smell of cooking.

'He's in the shed,' the keeper said. 'I was going to build him a pen. See those bricks over there? I was going to use them. Make him comfortable.'

'Well, that's not possible,' she said. 'He has to go back. Pigs can't live forever, anyway. I know it's sad – I know that. Yes, I do.'

Pig Twenty looked at them with interest. He had been lying on the heap of sacking and he rose to his feet when the door was opened. He stared at them for a moment and then he looked beyond them, at the garden beyond, his snout twitching.

The keeper did not argue. He took the halter of twine from a nail on which it had been hanging and he slipped it round Pig Twenty's neck.

'You're going back,' he said. 'Time to go back.'

Pig Twenty looked up at him, as if searching for confirmation, and then walked out ahead of them, restrained by the twine. The keeper bent down and patted him on the back. 'Sorry,' he whispered. 'I'm very sorry.' She heard this, and she knew. It was, for her, a sign; that a man should feel such sympathy for a pig; that was a sign of gentleness.

They made their way back across the fields. There was sun on the hills, like gold; there was warmth in the air, the scent of gorse. She thought: *it's so strange, so strange. Walking across the fields with a pig. And with him.*

Halfway across, they stopped to rest. Pig Twenty

sat down and looked up at the sky, as if puzzled, floored, by its sheer immensity. He might have thought, if he thought at all: is there a place for pigs there? Is that for pigs?

She turned to face the keeper. He smiled at her. She reached out. She reached for his hand. He took it. They stood there. She was certain.

That of all people, it should be him; that took her aback. That the heart should settle on somebody like him; that surprised her. But she was so certain about it, so certain.

10

I dream of you

Angus was the god of love, and of youth too, and of dreams. All who saw him loved him; there were no exceptions. They would wait for him to pass by and they would ask him to send them a dream of the man or the woman who would be their lover, and he always did that; he never refused. And if the person who stopped him and asked him was a girl or a woman, she would get a kiss, and the kiss would become a bird, a small bird that would flutter around for a few moments and then would disappear somewhere on the wind, leaving those who had seen it to wonder whether they had imagined the whole thing.

There were many, of course, who would have loved to claim his heart, but although Angus was a lover of women it seemed that there was none who could keep him for herself. And women, of course, tried every trick they could think of to ensnare this good-looking young man, consulting old women, wise in such matters, for the secrets that they knew. Special recipes were dispensed – potions that were applied to the cheeks, to the breast, just above the heart of those who would make Angus fall in love with them, but none of these seemed to have any effect. Angus had a way of telling when such tricks were being employed and became elusive when he knew that this was being done; skipped lightly away, away from the clutches of women. He laughed then, and the sound of his laughter only made the women more heartsore over what they saw but could not have.

But then Angus glimpsed his love, and she had no need of any trickery, of any potion, to take his soul away from him and make it hers. This happened at night, when Angus was alone and in his house. It was late. There was just darkness and a small fire in his room, a fire that provided little light, for it was just embers. But Angus had finished his evening meal and was ready to sleep on

the couch that was his bed. This couch was cov-
ered with the skins of deer, softened so that they
might not irritate the skin; and there were the skins
of otters too, as smooth as the water in which they
played, and of other small creatures.

That night, while he was asleep, a young woman
came to him in his dreams. She was as real to him
as if he were awake, and he was immediately struck
by her profound beauty. But there was more to it
than that; he knew that she was the person with
whom he wished to be forever. He stretched out his
hand to bring her to his bed, but she smiled and
left him.

He awoke the next morning, the skins from his
couch on the ground, the cool air of the morning
upon him. He looked about the room, hoping to see
the girl who had come to him in the night, but there
was no sign of her; not a trace, not a shadow. He
stood there, silent, struck by the beauty of the
vision vouchsafed him in the night, and he remembered it so well, in such lovely detail.

His door opened, and the woman whose job it

was to make breakfast for Angus brought in a bowl
of food and milk for him to drink. She laid it by
his window and left, but Angus did not touch the
food. He looked out of the window, longing to see
the girl he had dreamed of; there was nobody. There
was no girl.

That evening he went to bed tired and hungry,
for he had not eaten all day, so preoccupied had he
been with the memory of the girl and her nocturnal
visit. 'You must come to me tonight,' he whispered.
'And this time you must stay.'

She came again, just as she had done the pre-
vious night, and she was as beautiful and beguiling
as he had remembered her to be. Again he reached
out his hand and asked her to come to his bed, but
again, although she stayed for a time and played
music for him, she did not come to him.

This happened every evening, and each day
Angus sat under a tree, lost in thought, wondering
how he might persuade this girl to stay with him
and become his wife. He could not understand why
he should be punished in this way; why when most

men, and most gods too, were able to have a real women to love them he was only given a woman who came to him in his dreams, a succubus.

Those who were around Angus were soon alarmed by his failure to eat and by his constant brooding.

'We must call a healer,' said one of the women. 'We really must. We cannot allow him to fade away before our eyes. We cannot allow his sickness to go untreated.'

A healer came. He laid the god bare upon the ground. He looked at him and placed his hands upon his brow and his stomach. He peered into his eyes and listened to the sound of his breathing. But he could see nothing in all of this that told him of any illness, and he shook his head. 'I cannot see what is wrong,' he said. 'He must be made to eat and drink.'

But Angus would not eat, or, if he did, he took very little food – just enough to stop the body from dying altogether. More healers were summoned, and there were very fine ones among them. These were healers who could make broken bones knit together, who could drive fevers from the body with their poultices and their herbs, who could even rouse those given up for dead. They were great men, but none of them was great enough to diagnose what was wrong with Angus. So they agreed that they would summon the finest healer in Ireland, a man called Fergne. He could look at the face of a person and say immediately what was wrong with him. He could also look at the smoke coming from the chimney of a house and tell how many sick people there were inside. He was very gifted.

Fergne looked at Angus, who was lying listlessly on his bed, and knew at once what was wrong. Leaning over Angus he whispered to him, 'You are sick from a love that you have lost. That is what is wrong with you. I can tell.'

Angus was astonished that this healer could diagnose his condition so quickly and he straight away confessed that this was indeed what was wrong with him. He described to Fergne the beauty of the woman who visited him in his dreams and told him of her talent at the playing of the bodhrán. He spoke of how her music lulled him to sleep at night; lulled to sleep, but sick at heart, knowing that she would not be there when daylight came. Fergne nodded as all this was being revealed. It was exactly what he had thought it would be. He knew.

'Your mother must be called,' he said. 'We shall speak to her and see whether she knows who this girl is.'

Boann came, rising from her river in a burst of spray. She was alarmed that her son was in such a serious condition.

'What is wrong with you?' she asked. 'They tell me that you are pining for some girl. Really! You're not fourteen any more.'

Angus turned away. His mother did not understand.

She looked at his attendants. 'So what do they expect me to do? I can't make you eat if you don't want to.'

Angus said nothing to his mother, but the women who were watching this asked her whether she would be able to make enquiries as to who the girl was.

'How am I to do that?' asked Boann, irritably. 'There are so many girls. I have no idea which one has been visiting my son. Really! Why don't you ask his father. This is a matter for him. Dagda. That's who his father is.' There was the movement of water; there was a ripple; she went.

Dagda was summoned. He came across the turf with his club across his breast and his dark eyes gazing. There was a wind that came with him and the cattle, frightened, ran away at his approach. This was the father.

'Well?'

'Your son. Angus. Your son.'

'Oh yes?'

'He has met a beautiful girl, but we cannot find her. We need your help. You can send people over to Bodb and see if he can find the girl who fits the description he has given us.'

Dagda looked up at the sky. 'Not easy,' he said.

'But you must. Otherwise he will die.'

Dagda turned away; he was thinking of something else.

'But he is your son!'

'Very well.'

And Dagda left and went back to his home. There he ordered his men to go to Bodb and ask him whether he could find this girl. They went.

'Of course,' said Bodb, 'I am delighted to be able to help Dagda, who is, after all, my father. But this request is somewhat odd, if I might say so. What do we have? We have some dream that Angus has had – or says he has had. In my experience, dreams are unreliable, and the lovers whom people see in their dreams, well . . . Put it this way, I'm not exactly convinced. Far from it.

'However, a request from Dagda is hardly something I can ignore, and so let's see what we can do. I must say I feel a bit sheepish saying to these men of mine, *Go and find a girl who looks like . . . etc., etc.,*

etc. It's highly unlikely, but there we are. So I shall try to be helpful and I shall send some people off and tell them to find this girl. There are, you know, a great number of pretty girls in this part of the world – and all of them would positively *devour* Angus. But let's see. *Nil desperandum.*'

The orders were given, and a small band of men went off to look for the girl described by Dagda's messengers. They interrogated people they met on the road; they talked to farmers in their fields; they climbed trees and looked out over the land. They searched intensively, and after a year or so they saw her.

'She is there,' said the messenger to Bodb. 'We found her. She is at Lough Bel Dracon. That is where she is.'

'Well, I must say that I'm very pleased,' said Bodb. 'This is a remarkable achievement and there is no question but that Dagda will be overjoyed. And Angus, of course, will be relieved to hear about this. Or so we may assume. Sometimes the reality is not quite so appealing as the vision, distinctly so, but let's not be pessimistic. Go and fetch Angus and bring him to me.'

Angus came to Bodb, riding in a chariot lent him by Dagda. And the chariot went past the houses of young women who ran out to see him, feet bare, their hair streaming in the wind of his passing. To each he dispensed a kiss – to this side, to that – and passed on his way, leaving those he left behind him feeling elated, but sad, too, that they had seen him for so brief a time. To some of them he gave the gift of love – they would see in dreams that night the love that was destined for them; to others he gave the gift of youth – their step would be lighter that day, less burdened by the years.

And when he came to Bodb's place, at the end of his journey, his host awaited him, beaming. 'Well, Angus,' said Bodb. 'Dear brother – of sorts. Here you are. The end of your journey.'

Angus stepped down from his chariot. The horses that had pulled him were foamy with heat, nostrils dilated. They had travelled a great distance.

'Take the horses away,' said Bodb, waving a hand. 'Horses away! And here, Angus, come with me to the place where you will stay. Over here – see what we have prepared for you. Such a couch! And this evening, once you have rested, a bit of a celebration. A feast. Food. And music, too. Dancing, if you will. See.'

'I am most grateful,' said Angus. 'And Dagda, my father . . .'

'Will be grateful too,' said Bodb. 'Yes, of course. Dagda. One would want his gratitude. What with that great club of his. Certainly one would not want his enmity.'

'But what I would really like to do,' said Angus, 'is to find the girl who you say is here. I have been waiting for her.'

Bodb smiled. 'All in good time, Angus. All in good time. For the moment we're thinking of two or three days of feasting and merriment. Then we shall take you to the place that my men have identified. That's where this girl is to be found.'

It was hard for Angus to wait; he had already

waited over a year – a year of dreams and longing. 'I would like to see her now,' he said. But he was too tired to argue.

'No. Feast first, then the girl. That's what we have in mind.'

Angus retired to rest. He was tired after the journey, which had been a long one, but he found he could not sleep. He was afraid that should he sleep, he would find that the girl would not come to him in his dreams, now that he was so close to her. And so he stayed awake, lying wide-eyed, staring up at the smoky turf roof of the room into which Bodb had shown him.

At some point in the afternoon, while he was lying in his room, Angus saw a face peering in at him through the single small window above his bed. He gave a start: how long had he been observed? It is a shock to find out that we have been watched, and he felt unsettled by the discovery.

'Who are you?' he challenged. 'What are you doing?'

It was Bodb. 'Only me,' he said. 'Just looking.'

Angus wondered whether he could trust his host, but he told himself that it was unlikely that Bodb, who knew that he was the son of Dagda, would attempt any treachery. And so he continued to lie on his couch, and when evening came he went out to join Bodb at the large table which he had set out under a tree nearby.

Bodb had invited his friends, gods and people, and they made a rowdy company. Angus sat at the head of the table, next to Bodb, who poured him fermented juice and placed a plate of meat before him.

Bodb looked at Angus; he was interested. 'I must say you're persistent,' he remarked. 'I would never search for somebody as you've done. Remarkable. I suppose that love is like that. It obsesses one.' He paused. 'That's difficult to grasp – or at least it's difficult for me to understand. Why should anybody be so driven to possess another? Why? Loneliness? Is that it?'

He did not give Angus time to answer. 'But loneliness is easily dealt with. Look at all these people milling around. How can one be lonely when there are so many people? It can't be simple loneliness; it must be something more than that – a yearning, perhaps. Yes, that's what it is – a yearning to *be* the beloved, to enter into that other skin. Strange. Very strange. But why, may I ask, should men wish in this way to be women, and the other way round? Is it because the man feels that there is something missing in his world, and that he will never be complete until he has found that missing thing, which is being a woman. Is that it?'

The guests were silent now, watching Bodb. Each time he answered one of his own questions they nodded their agreement.

Angus spoke. 'It is the search for beauty,' he said. 'That is what it is. We find ourselves on this earth – gods and men – and we know that it is beautiful. That is one of the few things we understand – beauty; because it is there, in the world, and we can see it all about us. We want beauty. It requires our love. It just does.'

Bodb stared at him. 'I see. But once you have

found this girl, what then? You may have glimpsed perfect human beauty, but what then? Do you really think that you can possess the beauty of another? You can't, you know.'

At this, the assembled company shook their heads in agreement with Bodb. Angus said nothing. He would sit through this feast as a matter of courtesy to his host, but he did not have to agree with all that he said, even if it was true.

Bodb continued. 'Why, do you think, should people imagine that beauty and goodness go together? Do you think they do? I don't. Beauty can exist alongside the most appalling character defects. Vanity, in particular. But then, when we see pure beauty unsullied by such failings, it certainly does appear good to us.'

He looked at Angus, who in his turn was looking at a row of small gods who were gnawing at the bones of cattle. They glanced back at him and smiled, gesturing that he should join them in their feast. But Angus did not wish to eat: he wanted only to find the girl who had eluded him for so long.

Once he had found her, then he would eat.

Bodb was concerned. 'Love-sickness is a terrible thing,' he said. 'Look at you! Sitting there and not a morsel of food passing your lips.'

Angus hung his head. 'I'm sorry. It's difficult to eat and drink when one's mind is somewhere else.'

Bodb shrugged. 'I hope this girl is not a disappointment. I hope that she's not a wild bird or something like that.'

Angus showed his alarm. 'She is a girl. I have seen her.'

'Fine,' said Bodb. 'I'm sorry I mentioned it.'

At the end of the feasting, Bodb suggested to Angus that they should make their way together to the place where the girl had been spotted by his men.

'All we can do at this stage,' he said, 'is to make sure that she is indeed the one. That's all. I can't give her to you – you know that?'

Angus nodded. 'She will presumably have a father.'

'Exactly,' said Bodb. 'Fathers are a bit of a stumbling block. How many love affairs have fallen at that hurdle? Countless.' He reached out and touched Angus on the shoulder. 'But don't worry. I have a feeling that this will work out.'

Angus wanted to believe Bodb, but now he felt only doubt, and this doubt made him miserable. But he followed Bodb, along paths and tracks that led this way and that. Finally they came to a lough, and there, at the edge of the water, were three groups of girls. Angus stood quite still. The girl he had been looking for was there; she was there, and she stopped his heart.

Bodb stood beside Angus. 'Is that the girl? That one? The tall one?'

Angus could not speak. The girl seemed more perfect than she had been in his dreams – her features more delicate, her hair more golden, her laughter more sweet. He thought, *I love you so very much, so very much*, and she turned as he thought this and she could see that it was him and she blushed.

Bodb saw that Angus was transfixed, and for a while he did not speak to him, not wanting to intrude. But then he leaned forward and whispered into his ear, 'That's Caér. The daughter of Ethal Anbúail. Not within my gift, I'm afraid.' It saddened him to give Angus this news, but he had warned him that this was how things would probably turn out.

Angus turned away disconsolately and began his journey home. Bodb did not go home; he travelled all the way to see Dagda to report to him on what had happened; he did not trust Angus to speak to his father about the girl, as he had been loath to do so in the beginning and would not change.

'The girl,' said Bodb. 'The very girl.'

'So,' said Dagda. His thoughts were elsewhere.

'Father problems,' said Bodb.

'Oh yes.'

Bodb was diplomatic. 'An unhelpful father would not go over there and sort this thing out,' he said tentatively. 'But a father like you, Dagda, with a reputation for helpfulness, would do something.'

'Oh yes?'

'Yes. You would go over to the locals down there

— 145 —

– Ailill and Medb, I believe – and have a word with them. That's what somebody as conscientious as you would do.'

After that, Dagda could hardly decline to do something. He took a large number of his men with him and went to speak with Ailill, who proved to be very co-operative. He summoned him and asked Ailill to give the girl to Dagda for his son, Angus. The request was passed on to the girl's father, who was as unhelpful as Ailill had proved co-operative.

'Certainly not,' he said. 'I shall not hand over my daughter. Even to Angus. Certainly not.'

He was threatened, and this worked. But there was still a difficulty: Caér, it transpired, spent alternate years as a wild swan. If Angus wished, though, he could visit the lough where she was to be seen, and he could ask her then if she would go off with him.

Angus crept down to the edge of the lough. It was morning, and the air was fresh with the scent of wild flowers and fresh grass. Above him the sky was

open, empty, so blue that one might think that it
was water; below him were the fields and hedges,
the mounds that were entrances to the otherworld,
the paths that were for human feet and the feet of
cattle. He stood before an intricate spiderweb, out-
lined with droplets, and pushed aside its stanchions
with his chest; he frightened a hare upon a rock and
sent it bounding; he was watched by hawks, circling high above, who knew who he was, and followed him. And so he came to the lough where there
were clusters of swans, and of these swans one wore
gold chains about her neck, one was more beautiful.

Angus stood upon the shore. He stretched out
his arms, and they were wings, great swan-wings,
white to the pinions; he became a swan. She saw
him, turning her neck as swans will do, and he flew
to her. Then together they rose above the waters
of the lake and circled its shore several times. The
sound of their beating wings was the sound of a
heartbeat, the sound of blood in the veins, the very
sound of life; and they rose, and flew away to the
north, to be together, lovers as swans, as man and

woman; Angus, giver of dreams and love, now the recipient of both. Their wings are white against the blue; they are gone now, the clouds have taken them, they are gone.

Swans. There were two life-size swans, cast in bronze, which the sculptor had placed so that they seemed to rise up from a small grass-covered mound. It was as if they were helping one another into flight, the tips of their wings touching, their necks stretching out, fluid, in upward motion. Canadian Tundra Swans. Behind the sculpture, across an expanse of lawn, was the house itself.

The wonderful thing about the house was its position, right on the lake. In summer it was largely concealed by the trees behind it, so that if one approached from the direction of the road, the direction of the small town, it was as if there were no house there at all — just trees and a silver glimmer of water behind the foliage.

'The important thing about a cottage,' the architect had said, 'is that it should be as unobtrusive as possible. The very best effect we can achieve is that one might be walking through the bush and then – *voilà* – there it is, right in front of you, a surprise. That shows respect for the surroundings.'

'Yes. That's what we want isn't it?'

Sean had turned to her, and she had nodded her agreement. 'As long as it's not too small,' she said. 'I want light. Lots of light. I don't want something so hidden away that it's gloomy. Dark. No.'

The architect reassured her that there would be light – lots of it. 'You'll have falling light,' he said. 'Quite apart from the light from those large windows – and they will be large – you'll have light from skylights.'

Sean said, 'Falling light is very beautiful.'

The architect nodded. 'It is.' He paused. 'This place is going to be marvellous. Believe me. You're going to be very happy.' He beamed at them, as if bestowing a benediction. But he had been wrong; they were not happy there, because it was only two months after the cottage was completed and they had made their first trips out there for the weekend that she discovered about his affair, in their house in Toronto, on an ordinary Saturday morning.

She held the letter away from her, as if it were a dangerous object, a source of pollution. 'This letter,' she said.

He had been perched on the edge of his desk, which is how he liked to sit when he was paging through one of the books in his collection. He liked to pick a book off the shelf, at random, and read a few pages before putting it back and taking out another.

He looked up from the book. He had been elsewhere, lost, and had not heard what she had said. She was just holding a piece of paper, in his view; not the evidence of his guilt.

'Here's a good final sentence for a book,' he said. 'Listen to this, *And the driverless train rushed on, the passengers all singing lustily.* What an ending. You'd think . . .'

'This letter,' she repeated. 'I was looking in your jacket pocket for something.'

She felt that she did not have to explain that she

had come across it by accident; that she had not been searching for evidence. And how could she have been doing that, given that she had entertained no doubts until two minutes ago?

'In my pockets . . .' he began, and left the sentence unfinished.

She moved towards him and began to pass him the letter, but did not, and inadvertently dropped it to the floor. He put the book down on the desk and reached forward to retrieve the letter. His movement knocked the book off the edge of the desk and it fell to the ground, the cover open.

He ignored the book and picked up the letter. He folded it and tucked it into the pocket of his shirt.

'Well . . .' he began. He was looking at the floor, not at her.

'I suppose people still feel the need to write letters like that,' she said. 'A letter is like a kiss, isn't it? Like an act of love. Something you want to keep.'

She looked at him. He was flushed. His collar, she noticed, had a small spot of blood on it where he had nicked himself while shaving that morning. Previously that would have evoked a feeling of pity, at his blood, his dear blood; now it was revulsion. The physical.

'How could you?' Her voice was a whisper; he might not even hear her. 'How could you? Sean . . .'

He said nothing. He could not look at her, and she saw this.

'You're meant to be a Catholic. Some Catholic.' It was childish, but it was the first thing that came into her mind; to call on God, to threaten him – that was what she wanted to do. She had no other weapon. Church, State, loyalty; each of these capable of its particular outrage. These were the things that kept people together in the face of everything; we invoked them, desperately, when we knew that there was nothing else, no love.

He looked up sharply. 'What's that got to do with it?'

'Everything.'

Then she turned and walked out. She went into the kitchen and opened a drawer and slammed it shut again – a pointless action, the type of action carried out in blind haste when we do not know what to do, but have to act to escape the pressing horror of ourselves. The girl; barely twenty-three. That was her – the one who had been helping him in his studio. Of course it was her.

She left the kitchen and went into the hall. Her coat was on one of the pegs. It was still early spring and there was a chill wind from the north; it had blown yesterday and again today. Tomorrow the wind would come from the south, they had said; a warm wind from America, blowing into Canada.

Her car was parked further down the street. It was a Saturday and people came and parked outside the house, uninvited; people who were going shopping on the busy road at the end and who could not park outside the shops. She always resented them, but they were just like her, she told herself; everyone we resent is ultimately just like us.

She drove to her sister's house; drove dangerously, through her tears, almost knocking down a man at the corner of Harbord, signalling to him that it was an error, that she had not wanted to kill him; and he had shouted at her, his face distorted with rage. Because we are cruel to one another, she thought.

Her sister, Imogen, was in. 'I was about to go . . .' she said, but paused. 'There's something wrong. Oh my God, there's something wrong. Is somebody dead?'

It was very like death, she thought, over the next six months; it was such an ending. She did not go back to the house, but sent her sister to collect her possessions. There were a couple of conversations on the telephone – brief, taut events in which practicalities were discussed. He did not ask her back, he just said, 'Well, it's happened. But if this is what you want, then . . .' She would have liked him to ask her to return so that she could refuse, but he did not. She thought about that: he had his pride, he had always had it. And of course there would be that girl; he had her.

Her sister accepted her presence with her usual generosity. The issue was just not discussed; she had arrived and it was assumed that she would stay. There was plenty of room; she had a house in a quiet street, a house with four bedrooms and a glassed-in garden room that had been extended out at the back. There was green light that came into this room through the filter of the trees in the garden – a dappled, calming light. She liked to sit there in the evenings and read, while Imogen got on with her social and political life. Imogen played bridge on two evenings a week with a group of women, all in their mid-thirties. On the other evenings she went to meetings of the various causes in which she was involved. There was a literacy trust that raised money for reading schemes; there was an environmental pressure group that scrutinised development plans; there was a fund for democracy. There were obscure causes that were to do with refugees and prisoners of conscience. They organised chains of help at the end of which there was real suffering, real people in prison. 'The world is such a cruel place,' said Imogen. 'We don't see it here. We're lucky. But . . .'

'Yes. You're right.'

Imogen sighed. 'And all we can do is hold another coffee morning.'

'It's something.'

'I feel so guilty,' Imogen went on. 'So helpless.'

'You shouldn't.'

She might have involved herself in Imogen's world, but did not. That would have required commitment, belief – things that she now felt she simply did not have. She had believed in things when she was with him; they had believed in the world together; now that seemed to have gone.

She spent hours thinking about him, going over the pathology of their relationship, from the very start. How could he have lied to her? Because there must have been lies. The working lunches that must have been social, must have been trysts; the weekend when he had had to go to Montreal and had dissuaded her from coming with him. 'It's going to be a boring photo shoot, that's all. You'll be twiddling your thumbs. Far better to stay at home.' Lies; all lies.

She saw his work from time to time in magazines – he was one of the most successful photographers in the country, in all of North America, really. She turned the pages quickly when this happened, as the images were too painful. *This is what his eye has seen*, she thought. *This is him looking at the world.*

'You'll have to get a job one of these days,' Imogen said. 'I don't like to interfere – you know that – but you can't do nothing. Nobody can do nothing.'

'I've got enough money.'

'But it's not money. No. It's the . . . well, I'm sorry to say it, it's the sitting around. You've got to get some sort of hold of your life.'

That had brought tears, copious tears, and Imogen had felt guilty and had tried to comfort her. And at the end of the discussion which followed, she had agreed with Imogen that the first thing she could do in sorting out her life was to see a therapist.

'I know it sounds self-indulgent,' said Imogen, 'but seeing somebody can really help you to get over something like this. It . . . it sorts things out in your mind. It really does.'

'But who?'

'There's a man who practises from his house in the Annex. I know a few people who have been to him. They swear by him, they really do.'

She had agreed at least to try. It had never occurred to her before that she would end up going to a therapist; that was something that other people did – neurotic people, people who could not cope with their lives. People who sat about all day. Me, she thought.

'Well, I went,' she said to Imogen. 'I went to see this person of yours. Proud of me?'

'I am, actually. It takes a bit of courage to go. Yes, I am proud of you.'

She laughed. 'It was very easy. The hour went very quickly.' She paused. Imogen was writing one of her lists; a list of meetings or people to write to about one of the causes, or a plan of attack on a local politician. There were many lists. 'Have you met him?'

'Never.'

'He's rather appealing. Not a fuddy-duddy with a beard – which is what I expected – but a young man. Athletic. Energy.'

'Good.'

'And his eyes . . . There's something about them. Really quite remarkable. Intelligent – really intelligent – but rather mischievous.'

'Sexy?'

'Dead sexy.'

Imogen looked up from her list. She laid her pencil down on the table. 'Don't,' she said. 'Just don't.'

'Don't what?'

'You know very well what I mean. Don't fall in love with your therapist. Rule number one.'

She laughed. 'I have no intention. None at all. I was just describing him to you, that's all.'

She told Imogen of what had happened. She had

been tearful at first, she said, when she had told him about it, and he had sat there, nodding. How many times had he heard all that before? Presumably every second patient had the same story. Love and its disappointments were the bread and butter of people like him.

But then he had said to her, 'I should tell you that I'm fairly eclectic in my approach. I'm an analyst, you know, but I don't necessarily work that way with everyone, and I'm not sure if psychoanalysis is what you want, or need at the moment. But what I do a lot of – and many people find it very helpful – is dream work. We look at dreams and see what they have to tell us. You know about that?'

'A bit.' She had had a friend who was writing a thesis on Freudian theory and she had talked about it. It seemed quite reasonable – that dreams should tell us what we really want to do. That had never struck her as being a particularly revolutionary insight.

He continued. 'In particular, I'm interested in

lucid dreaming. And it may be that we might do something there. Have you ever had a lucid dream?'

'I don't know what a lucid dream is.'

'It's quite simple, really. It's where you have a dream but it's an unusual sort of dream. In ordinary dreams, what happens to you is quite real to you. Your experience at the time is no different to your normal experience; what happens to you really happens, while you're dreaming, at least. That's why nightmares are so terrifying – it's really happening.'

She looked past him, through the window. There were leaves against the sky, just moving in the breeze; there were a few white clouds. A small bird landed on the windowsill, briefly, its little feet slipping on the paintwork, and then it flew off again. He looked.

Turning back to her: 'A lucid dream is quite different. In a lucid dream, you know that you're dreaming. Yes, you do. You know that it's a dream and this gives you great power, because you can control what happens. Have you had a dream like that before?'

She thought for a moment, and then she remembered. She had, although she had not known the name for them. There had been lucid dreams – often.

'Flying.'

He looked interested. 'Yes?'

'I have these dreams in which I can fly – I think lots of people do, don't they? I know at the time that it's just a dream, but I still fly. I suppose that I think *I can still fly, because it's a dream.*'

He had seemed pleased with this. 'That's exactly it. And it suggests that you're a good subject.'

'A good subject for what?'

He had leaned forward and picked up a paper clip from his desk. Now he unbent the metal, straightening it. 'We can use your dreams to help you,' he said.

She met his gaze, and then looked away. The chair in which she was sitting was near a wall, and by turning her neck slightly she saw the framed diploma immediately above her. There was a press cutting, yellowed with age; something about a victory in a long-distance run. There were photographs too, old photographs, sepia, black and white: one caught her eye – a man, a woman, a boy outside a harbour, a ship behind them, in the background, a long time ago. A long time ago. The woman's arm was around the boy's shoulder; she was smiling; the boy was looking off to the side at something outside the camera's view. Where was this? She saw, written in pencil beneath it, the inscription *Halifax, 1934*. So long ago. She looked back at him. He was watching her; *he has kind eyes*, she thought. *He is very kind.*

They agreed the treatment plan. She would come to him four times a week for the next few weeks and they would see how things went. He asked her to write down such dreams as she remembered immediately after waking. Then they would discuss these, and other things too. 'We'll feel our way through it,' he said. 'Just be relaxed about it. Don't worry.'

She remembered a few dreams and wrote them down in her notebook. She told him, 'I was cooking something or other. It was a large kitchen, a bit like my sister's kitchen. Somebody was coming to dinner – one of Imogen's friends, I think. I spilled something on the table. That's about it, I'm afraid.'

He seemed to be interested even in this fragment, but they did not discuss it. Then at the next session she said, 'I dreamed about my husband.'

He said, 'Not a lucid dream?'

She looked down at the floor. She was ashamed. 'No, I don't think so. He was in the house – Imogen's house – and I told him that he shouldn't be there. He took no notice. He was fiddling with something, and I couldn't see what it was. He just ignored me, and I felt very angry.'

He was interested in this, and they discussed it at some length. It was important, he said, because her husband's departure had precipitated this crisis for her – that was agreed, wasn't it? – and therefore his appearance in a dream was significant. Her feelings about him were coming through now – the pain of rejection, the angry response – all that was quite normal, and it was healthy that it should do so. 'It's a release,' he said. 'It shows movement.'

But then he said to her, 'We have something else to do — something that will be far more useful than merely working out what is, after all, pretty obvious stuff. You have to engage with your husband in the dream. I want you to try to have a lucid dream about him.'

'But surely I can't tell myself what I'm going to dream.'

'Yes, you can. We are very open to suggestion. Tell yourself *I'm going to dream about him, and I'm going to know it's a dream.* Tell yourself that. Try.'

'And what should I do? If I can control the dream, what should I do? Fly?'

He smiled. 'No. I think that you should make him say sorry to you. Make him do that in the dream.'

She was silent. She sat there for a moment, and then she felt the tears in her eyes. He had not said sorry. I loved him so much, and I thought he loved me. But he has hurt me, hurt me. And he has not said sorry. Not once.

'I don't know if I'll be able to do it.'

He said, 'Try.'

At first it did not work. Before she went to bed she willed herself to dream, and to be aware of the dream, but the dreams she had were ordinary dreams – there was no consciousness of the fact that the normal self, the waking self, was there. She told him that she had tried to no avail, and he said, 'Persist. Just persist.' And then, a week later, she had a lucid dream, and the dream's recipe was exactly what she had willed. He was there, this time with his camera in his hand, standing in front of her. She knew now that she was in control; she could make him do in the dream what she wanted him to do. But he did not speak, and she found herself feeling puzzled.

'That's still good progress,' said the therapist. 'Persist.'

There was nothing, but then a vivid dream came, and it was lucid. This time she had the therapist at her side, in the dream, and he was holding her hand. 'Make him do what you want him to do,' he whispered to her.

She looked at her husband. 'Why didn't you say sorry to me?' she said. 'You ruined . . . you ruined everything.' She was on the verge of tears. But she found that she could stop herself from crying; she was in control.

Her husband cast his eyes down. 'I'm very sorry,' he said. 'I was sorry from the beginning. I'm just a man.'

She turned to the therapist. 'Did you hear that?' she said triumphantly. 'Did you hear that? He said he's just a man.'

'So am I,' said the therapist. And then, quite unexpectedly, he began to fly.

She told him about the dream at their next session. He listened carefully, and laughed at the description of his flying.

'I'd like to leave it for a little while,' he said. 'I have to be away for the next four weeks. I'm going to Vancouver for training. You should come and see me when I come back, but in the meantime I want you to think about what happened in that dream. I want you to let it settle in your mind. Let it do its work.'

She felt out of sorts over the next few days, finding that she missed the sessions. 'Dependence,' said Imogen. 'You have to watch out for that.'

She tried to think of other things. She went to some of Imogen's meetings, but found that she came back from them depressed. There was so much wrong with the world, so much suffering, but she could not work up the sense of outrage that her sister so clearly felt. She slipped out of some of the meetings, going off to bookstores which stayed open in the evening, drinking coffee and paging through books. She started to read again, which was a good sign, she thought. I'm getting better.

She dreamed of her husband again. In this dream, which was vivid, even if not lucid, she was looking at him through some sort of window. He was standing on the other side of the glass, and when she opened it he put out his hand and took hers. He wept. 'I wanted you to come to me,' he said. 'I didn't dare ask.'

The dream stayed with her that day, and she wrote it down so that she could discuss it with her therapist when he returned from Vancouver. *I wanted you to come to me*, she wrote.

She found herself wondering about him now. Had the girl moved in with him after she had moved out? Did they live together in the house that she had chosen with him, that they had furnished together? She had no answers to these questions.

But then, one afternoon, she was driving in that part of town – and she had tried to avoid it before now – and she thought, *It would be easy for me to turn right at the next corner and drive down that street, to the house we lived in*. She slowed down. The intersection was drawing closer; a car behind her moved out impatiently and overtook. The driver, a thickset man, looked at her rudely and muttered something to himself. She ignored him.

Now she was at the intersection, and she

turned. The car obeyed. Down the street. Further. And then she stopped, half a block away, where she could see the house. It was a Saturday afternoon. He would be in. If she waited here, sitting in the car, she might see him coming out and then she might see him with her, walking down the street. Her heart raced, but she had decided now.

She turned on the radio. The car was parked in a shady place, but it was still warm inside, the sort of day that was in-between seasons. She listened to the radio. There was a discussion between politicians; they were bickering, accusing one another of bad faith. She changed stations until she heard music, restful music, something classical and restrained.

She looked at her watch. It was four o'clock. He often went out shortly before five. He was regular in his walking habits, like Immanuel Kant, he said; just like Immanuel Kant in Königsberg. She closed her eyes. She felt drowsy.

She fought sleep, as she wanted to stay awake,

now that she was here. But it came over her, like a blanket, and she dozed, and dreamed. She dreamed the same dream; that he was standing in front of her and that she was looking at him through a window. I'm dreaming, she thought. This is a dream. I am in my car and this is a dream.

But then she opened her eyes and he was looking at her through the window of the car. He was standing outside, looking through the car window.

She fumbled with the switch. She did not even think about it – she did that automatically. And the window started to wind down.

He stretched out his hand to her, through the window.

'I wanted you to come to me,' he said. 'I didn't dare ask.'

She began to weep. He too. They were tears of relief, sorrow, forgiveness.

★   ★   ★

DREAM ANGUS

Will he come to me, Dream Angus,
Come quietly through the evening light,
Come when I do not expect him, and I am
   sleepy,
Come when I am drowsy, when I am ready for
   rest;
Will he come to me, Dream Angus?

He will come, my dear; he will come at just that
   time;
You will see him at your window, my dear,
He will be there — he always is.

Will I see the birds about his head,
The birds that are his kisses?
Will I believe that each of us,
Even he who thinks himself unloved,
May be transformed, made different
By one who finds him marvellous? Will I
   think that?

I DREAM OF YOU

Yes, you will think exactly that, just that,
When Angus comes to you; I promise,
I promise you that.

Will he bring me some sort of quietus,
Some form of understanding; will he break
   my heart;
Will he show me my love; will he give
Me heart's contentment, the end of sorrow,
Will he do that for me; will he do that?

Dream Angus will do that, my dear,
He will do that; you may sleep now,
For Dream Angus leaps light across the heather,
And the name upon his lips is your name,
And the gifts that he bears are gifts for you;
That is true, my dear, it is all true.

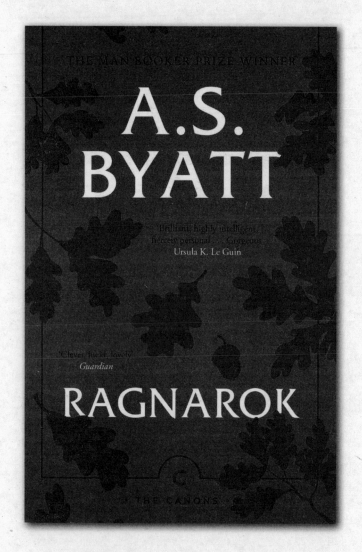

A.S. BYATT

'Brilliant, highly intelligent . . . fiercely personal . . . Gorgeous'
Ursula K. Le Guin

'Clever, lucid, lovely'
Guardian

RAGNAROK

THE CANONS

'Byatt's prose is majestic'
Sunday Telegraph

CANON‖GATE

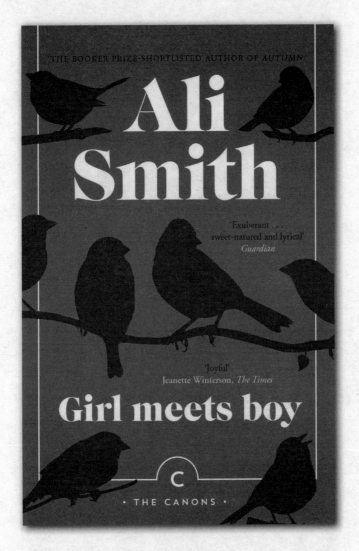

Ali Smith

'Exuberant . . .
sweet-natured and lyrical'
Guardian

'Joyful'
Jeanette Winterson, *The Times*

Girl meets boy

C

• THE CANONS •

'A glorious wide-awake dream of a book'
Observer

CANON❚❚GATE

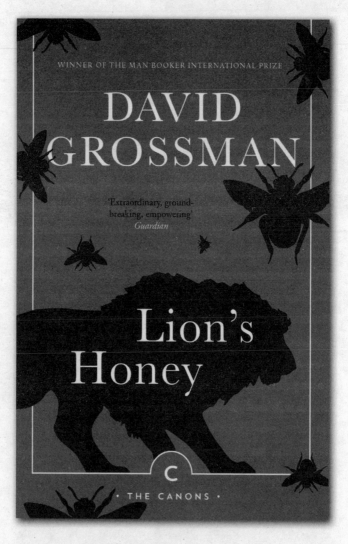

DAVID GROSSMAN

'Extraordinary, ground-
breaking, empowering'
Guardian

Lion's
Honey

· THE CANONS ·

'A master of the emotionally accurate
and significant' Yann Martel

CANON GATE